FRANÇOIS MAURIAC

FRANÇOIS MAURIAC

THE WEAKLING

and

THE ENEMY

TRANSLATED BY GERARD HOPKINS

FARRAR, STRAUS AND GIROUX

NEW YORK

THE WEAKLING was published in French under the title LE
SAGOUIN Copyright 1951 by Librairie Plon

THE ENEMY was published in French under the title LE MAL
Copyright 1935 by Editions Bernard Grasset
ISBN 0-374-52649-4

Library of Congress Catalog Card Number: 52-5923

Copyright 1952 by Pellegrini & Cudahy

THE WEAKLING

1

W HY go on saying that you know your lesson, when it's quite obvious that you don't? . . . . You just learned it off by heart, didn't you now?"

There was the sound of a slap.

"Go to your room, and don't let me set eyes on you till dinner-time!"

The child raised his hand to his face and felt it gingerly, as though his jaw had been broken.

"Ooh! that did hurt!" (he might as well make the most of his advantage) "I'll tell Mamie, you see if I don't! . . ."

In an access of fury, Paula grabbed her son's skinny arm, and administered a second slap.

"Mamie, eh? . . . well, here's something for you to go whining to your father about! . . . . what are you waiting for? . . . get out of my sight!"

She pushed him into the passage, shut the door, then opened it again to fling lesson books and notebooks after the retreating Guillaume. Still snivelling, he squatted down on his heels and picked them up. There was a sudden silence; not so much as the sound of a snuffle in the darkness. At last she had got rid of him!

She listened to his departing footsteps. It was pretty certain that he would not seek refuge with his father, and, since his grandmother, his "Mamie," was out, pleading his cause with the schoolmaster, it would be the kitchen he'd make for, to get a little sympathy from Fraülein. He was probably at it already, taking a surreptitious lick at the cooking food under the sentimental eyes of the Austrian woman. "I can as good as see him doing it. . . ." What Paula saw, when she thought about her son, was a picture of knock-knees, skinny legs, and socks festooned untidily over his shoes. This little scrap of humanity, this flesh of her flesh, had eyes the color of ripe blackberries, but of them she took no account. On the other hand, she was horribly conscious, with bitter loathing, of the sagging, adenoidal mouth and the drooling lower lip. It was less prominent than his father's, but it was enough for Paula that it reminded her of a mouth she hated.

Rage flooded her mind—rage?—or was it just exasperation? It is no easy thing to tell where exasperation ends and hate begins. She went back into the room, and paused for a moment in front of the wardrobe looking-glass. Each year, when autumn came round, she put on the same old knitted jersey of greenish wool which had grown too big for her round the neck. No amount of cleaning could keep the stains from reappearing. The brown skirt, spattered with mud, stuck out in front as though she were with child—though, thank God, there was no fear of that!

"Baronne de Cernès"—she muttered to herself—"the Baronne Galéas de Cernès. Paula de Cernès." Her lips parted in a smile which brought no gaiety to the bilious cheeks with their thick growth of down (the Cernès urchins made a great joke of Madame Galéas' whiskers!). She stood there, laughing to herself, and thinking of the girl she once had been who, thirteen years earlier, before another mirror, had stood nerving herself to take the plunge with repetition of the selfsame words: "The Baron and the Baronne Galéas de Cernès. . . . *M. Constant Meulière, sometime Mayor of Bordeaux, and Madame Meulière, take pleasure in announcing the marriage of their niece, Paula Meulière, to the Baron Galéas de Cernès.*"

Neither uncle nor aunt, eager though they were to be rid of her, had urged the taking of that lunatic step. They had even warned her against it. What school influence was it that had bred in her a weakness for titles?—to what pressure had she yielded? Today she could find no answer to that question. Perhaps mere curiosity had been the reason, or the longing to force an entry into a forbidden world. . . . She had never forgotten the groups of aristocratic children in the City Park—the Curzays, the Pichon-Longuevilles—in whose games there could never have been a question of her joining. The Mayor's niece had circled in vain about those arrogant scions of a nobler race. . . . "Mamma says we mustn't play with you. . . ." The grown girl had, no doubt, sought to avenge the snubbed child. Her marriage, she had thought, would open a way for her into the unknown, would be the harbor from which she could set sail for unimagined splendors. She knew all right today what people meant when they spoke of "closed circles": only too well she knew! To enter this one had seemed hard enough, almost impossible—but not so hard, not so impossible, as getting out of it again!

And for that she had thrown away her life! To have said she felt at moments a regret, would have been to indulge in understatement! Even obsession was too weak a word! Her

5

hideous fate had only too real a body. Never a moment passed but she was conscious of it. It was there to be seen, the embodiment of idiotic vanity, of criminal stupidity, the sign and symbol of an ineluctable destiny. To make matters worse, she was not even "Madame la Baronne." There was only one Madame la Baronne, her ancient mother-in-law. Paula would never be anything but Madame Galéas. Her imbecile husband's outlandish name had become her own, so that she was bound still closer, if that were possible, to the ruin she had married and made her own forever.

At night, the mockery of her life, the horror that came with the thought that she had sold herself for a golden vanity of which she could not enjoy even the shadow, filled her mind and kept her sleepless until morning. If she sought distraction in imagined fantasies—not seldom filthy—the rock-bottom of her thought remained immovable. All night long she lay in the darkness, struggling to clamber from the pit into which she had fallen of her own free will, knowing there was no escape. Whatever the season of year, night for her was always the same. In the Carolina poplars near the window the owls in autumn hooted to the moon like baying dogs, but they were infinitely less hateful than the implacable nightingales of spring. The sense of rage, of desperation at having been duped was always waiting for her when she woke, especially in winter, to the sound of Fraülein's heavy-handed drawing of the curtains. Emerging from the mists of sleep, she saw through the windows a few ghosts of trees, still hung with tattered leaves, waving their blackened branches in the eddying fog.

And yet, those were the best times of her day, those morning

6

moments when she could lie torpid in the snug warmth of the half-deserted bed. Little Guillaume was only too glad to forget the duty of the day's first kiss. Quite often Paula could hear, beyond the door, the voice of the old Baronne, urging the boy to go in and say good morning to his mother. Though she detested her daughter-in-law, she would make no compromise with principle. Then Guillaume would slip into the room and stand for a moment on the threshold, all eyes for the terrifying head upon the pillows with its hair drawn tightly back upon the temples to reveal a narrow, vaguely defined forehead, and a yellow cheek (with the mole nestling in a tuft of black hair) to which he would hastily press his lips. He knew in advance that his mother would wipe away the hasty salutation, and say, with disgust sounding in her voice, "You always make me so wet. . . ."

She no longer struggled against her feeling of disgust. Was it her fault that she could get nothing from the wretched creature? What could she do with a sly and backward child who always knew that his grandmother and old Fraülein would back him up? But now even the Baronne was growing sensible. She had agreed to see what she could do with the schoolmaster—an irreligious schoolmaster, to be sure, but that couldn't be helped. The curé had three parishes to serve, and lived over a mile away. On two separate occasions, once in 1917, and again in 1918, they had tried the experiment of boarding Guillaume away from home, first with the Jesuits at Sarlat, then at a small Seminary in the Lower Pyrenees. But he had been sent back after a term. The nasty little creature soiled his sheets. Neither the Jesuits, nor the Seminarists, were equipped, especially not just then, to deal with backward, or with sickly, boys.

The Weakling and the Enemy

How would this schoolmaster, with his curly hair and laughing eyes, a veteran of Verdun, welcome the old Baronne? Would he feel flattered that she had put herself out for him? Paula had managed to get herself excused. She lacked the courage now to face strangers, least of all this brilliant teacher. She was terrified of him. The Cernès bailiff, Arthur Lousteau, though a strong adherent of the *Action française,* was full of admiration for him, was convinced that he would go far. . . . The old Baronne, like all the country gentry, thought Paula, had a way with the "natives." She knew the subtleties of local patois. One of the few things about her which still had power to charm was the outworn elegance with which she spoke that ancient tongue. . . . Yes, but this socialist schoolmaster had other origins, and the Baronne's excessive affability might seem to him insulting. The affected pretense of seeming not to notice social differences no longer appealed to young men of his type. Still, after all, he had been wounded at Verdun, and that would create a bond with the old lady, whose younger son, Georges de Cernès had been reported "missing" in Champagne.

Paula opened the window, and saw, at the far end of the avenue, the Baronne's bent, emaciated figure. She was leaning heavily on her stick. A black straw hat was perched high on her piled hair. She moved between the elms which seemed ablaze, herself all glowing in the light of the setting sun. Paula could see that she was talking and gesturing. That she should be so agitated was no good sign. The young woman went down the great double staircase which was the glory of Cernès, and met her in the hall.

"A boor, my dear, as was only to be expected."

8

The Weakling and the Enemy

"Did he refuse? Are you sure you didn't rub him the wrong way? I do hope you didn't put on your grand manner . . . I told you . . ."

The elder lady shook her head, but her denial was only the automatic protest of the very old, which seems to be saying "No" to death. An artificial white flower trembled ludicrously on her straw hat. Her eyes were dim with tears which would not flow.

"What excuse did he make?"

"He said that he was too busy . . . that his work as the Mayor's secretary left him no leisure. . . ."

"He must have cooked up a better story than that. . . ."

"I assure you that he did not. He spoke only of his work. He didn't, he said, want anything to 'interfere with it'. . . ."

The Baronne de Cernès clung heavily to the banisters, and kept stopping for breath. Her daughter-in-law followed slowly, climbing the stairs behind her, questioning her all the time with that nagging obstinacy of which she was so little aware. She noticed, however, that she was frightening the old lady, and made an effort to lower her voice. But the words still hissed between her clenched teeth.

"Why did you say at first that he behaved like a boor?"

The Baronne sat down on the landing sofa. She was still shaking her head, and a grimace, which might have been a smile, was agitating her lips. Paula raised her voice again: had she or had she not accused the schoolmaster of boorishness?

"No, my dear, no . . . I was guilty of exaggeration. Maybe I misunderstood . . . Quite possibly the young man was innocent of intentional offense . . . I may have read meanings into his words which were not there."

9

But Paula would not desist. What meanings? What had he said?

"It was when he asked me why we had not applied to the curé. I told him that the curé does not live here, that he has three parishes on his hands. Do you know what that wretched schoolteacher had the effrontery to say? . . . but, no, it'll only make you angry . . ."

"What did he say? I won't give you a moment's peace until you tell me exactly what he said."

"Well, he told me with a snigger that on one point, it seemed, he saw eye to eye with the curé. Neither of them liked entanglements, and he certainly had no intention of getting himself mixed up with the great house. Oh, *I* knew well enough what he meant, and I would have you know that if he hadn't been wounded at Verdun, I would have made him explain himself more explicitly. *I'd* have known how to defend you!"

Paula's rage fell suddenly to silence. She hung her head, and, without another word, hurried downstairs, and took her cloak which was hanging in the hall.

The Baronne waited until the front door had closed behind her. This time there was no doubt about the smile which disclosed her discolored dentures. Leaning over the stair-rail, she spat out the three words—"*That* got you!", and then, in a cracked but piercing voice, cried out suddenly—"Galéas! Guillou!—darlings!"

She was not kept long waiting for an answer. It came from the remote depths of the service wing, from the kitchen: "Mamie! Maminette!" Father and son came dashing up the stairs, making no noise in their stockinged feet. Her call had meant that, for a time at least, the enemy had gone. They could get together now and sit round the lamp in Mamie's room.

Galéas took his mother's arm. He was wearing an old brown woolly. His shoulders were narrow and sloping, his disproportionately large head was covered with a great mat of hair. There was a childlike charm about his eyes, but the drooling, open mouth and thick tongue were horrible. His trousers hung loose above his feet, and sagged in great folds about his skeleton legs.

Guillaume had taken Mamie's other hand, and was rubbing his cheek against it. Of her words he retained only those that concerned him nearly. The schoolmaster didn't want to be bothered with him; he wouldn't have to stand trembling under those appraising eyes. The shadow of that particular monster was growing less. All else that Mamie had said was incomprehensible. "I got a good one in on your mother!"—A good one? What was that? The three of them entered the beloved room. Guillaume made for his corner between the *prie-Dieu* and the bed. In the back of the *prie-Dieu* there was a tiny cupboard filled with broken rosaries. One of them, with mother-of-pearl beads, had been blessed by the Pope: another, of olive stones, had been brought back by Mamie from Jerusalem. There was a metal box made in the shape of St. Peter's at Rome. It had been one of Galéas' christening presents, and bore his name in silver letters. There were prayer-books crammed with pictures showing the smiling features of the dead. Mamie and papa were whispering together under the lamp. A fire of logs threw vivid gleams into the corners of the room. Mamie took from the drawer in the pedestal table a greasy pack of tiny cards.

"We shan't be disturbed until dinner-time, Galéas: you can play the piano."

She was soon absorbed in her game of Patience. The piano had been brought into this room, filled though it was to bursting with assorted furniture, because Paula could not bear to listen to her husband's strumming. Guillaume knew in advance what the tunes would be. His father would play them in exactly the same order. First, the *Turkish Patrol*. Every evening Guillou waited for the same wrong note in the same place. Sometimes Galéas would talk while he was playing. His toneless voice sounded as though it were still at the breaking stage.

"This schoolmaster's a red, isn't he, mamma? As red as red —at least, that's what Lousteau says."

The *Turkish Patrol* resumed its uncertain course. A picture rose before Guillaume's eyes of the red man all smeared with ox blood. Not that he didn't know him well by sight—a limping figure, always bareheaded, and leaning on a handsome ebony cane. The red must be hidden by his clothes. Red like a fish. The last of the daylight still showed between the drawn curtains. Mamma would go wandering about the country till dinner-time, as she always did when she was in a particularly bad temper. She would come back, hatless, with mud on the bottom of her dress. She would smell of sweat. As soon as dinner was over, she would go to bed. They would be able to have a good hour together in front of Mamie's fire. Fraülein came in, tall and fat and flabby. She always found some excuse to join them when the enemy was out tramping the roads. Would they like their chestnuts boiled or roasted? Had she better do an egg for Guillou? She brought with her into grandmamma's room a mixed smell of onions and washing-up. This asking of her employers' wishes was a pure formality. Guillou would have his egg . . . (he had been so called since the war on account of his being unlucky enough to have the same name as the Kaiser—or "késer" as the Baronne pronounced it).

Already they were talking of "her." "She told me my kitchen was dirty . . . so I said that I was mistress in my own kitchen. . . ." Guillaume could see Mamie and papa stretching their skinny necks, the better to hear what Fraülein was saying. To him it was of no interest whatever, since for other people he felt neither hate nor love. His grandmother, his father, Fraülein provided that climate of security which he found so necessary, from which his mother fought tooth and nail to drive him, like a ferret attacking a rabbit deep in its warren. At no matter what cost, he had got to come out, and, dazed, bewildered, submit to her furious rages. When that happened he just rolled himself into a ball and waited for the storm to pass. Thanks, however, to the state of warfare that was forever smoldering between the grown-ups, he could, to some extent, live his life in peace. He hid behind Fraülein. The Austrian woman spread over him a bulky shadow of protection. Mamie's bedroom might be a safer refuge than the kitchen, but he knew better than to trust Mamie, or to rely upon the kindness of her words and gestures. Fraülein was somebody apart. With a love that was half a passion of the flesh, she brooded over her chick, her duckling. She it was who gave him his bath, and soaped him with her old hands, which were so chapped and dirty.

The Weakling and the Enemy

Meanwhile, Paula had turned into the path which led off to the left from the front steps. She reached, unseen, a narrow lane behind the stableyard. It was almost always deserted. She strode along it like a man. As a rule she went nowhere, but this evening her progress was marked by a strange air of haste. Walking, she could the more easily chew over the words spoken by the schoolmaster, and told her by her mother-in-law, those veiled references to the gossip about her and the late curé. The knowledge that she, and none but she, had built the prison in which she now lived, was ever a horror with her. It might have been tolerable—or so she thought—but for the shame that had fallen upon her during the first year of her married life. Inevitably she was a branded criminal in the eyes of all who saw her. She had been made to bear the burden of a fault which she had not committed, of a fault that was not so much shameful as ridiculous. For once it was not her husband, or his mother, who was responsible for the ill-natured gossip. Her real enemies lived in a world where vengeance could not reach them. Only at an occasional religious ceremony had she so much as seen them at a distance—those Vicar-Generals, those Canons of the Church in whose eyes the daughter-in-law of the Baronne de Cernès was a walking danger to the spiritual health of all anointed priests. The scandal was a matter of common knowledge throughout the diocese. It was bandied from mouth to mouth. Already there had been three successive chaplains at Cernès, and each had been reminded by the diocesan authorities that permission to say Mass in the private chapel had been rescinded; that, though there must be no open scandal, they must be careful to avoid familiar discourse

14

The Weakling and the Enemy

with the family (for all its great name) "because of a scandal that is only too well known to all of us."

For several years now, because of Paula, the Chapel at Cernès had been left unconsecrated. That in itself was a matter of complete indifference to the young woman (the distance of the Parish Church had provided her with a blessed excuse for never setting foot in it). But there was not a person within ten miles who did not know why that interdict had been laid upon the family. It was because of the old lady's daughter-in-law— "her as had been caught with the curé." The more indulgent gossipers would add that, actually, no one knew precisely how far things had gone. Probably they had not done anything really *wrong* . . . all the same . . . well, the priest had been sent away, hadn't he?

The tree trunks were in shadow, but a streak of red still lay low against the sky. It was long since Paula had noticed such things—trees, the sky, the wide stretches of the countryside, though, at times, like any peasant, she would read the signs in nature of a coming storm, of a change in the temperature. Once she had found pleasure in the visible world, but all that part of her had died on the day when, at this very hour, and on this selfsame road, she had walked beside an overgrown innocent, a young, half-famished priest. He had been pushing his bicycle and talking to her in a low voice. The peasants who had seen them pass had had no doubt that love was the burden of their words. But all that had ever happened had been the meeting, in their persons, of two solitary sufferers whose loneliness had never mingled.

Paula had heard the laughter of a group of girls and boys behind a turning in the road. In a moment they would be in

15

sight. She had pressed into the bank so as not to see them, so as not to be seen. She had led her companion into a track which branched off from the lane. It had been a foolish thing to do, because it had at once given rise to suspicion.

This evening, though a damp mist was rising, she sat down among the dead leaves of a chestnut copse, drew her knees up to her chin, and clasped her hands about her legs. Where was he now, that poor young priest? Where was he hiding his suffering? She did not know, but only that, wherever he might be, he would be suffering if he were still alive. No, there had never been anything between them. It was not the thought of *that* which worried her. Brought up in the horror of the priestly habit, such an intrigue would have been for her impossible. Yet, the poor imbeciles who lived about had classed her—and with authority to back them—among those mad and sex-starved women who make themselves a burden to the clergy. Nothing she could do would ever tear that label from her neck. But what of him? Had he in any way been guilty? He had responded to the confidences of a young, despairing woman, not with the grave words of a spiritual director, but with confidences returned. That had been the sum-total of his wrongdoing. She had sought help from him, as she had had a perfect right to do—and he had welcomed her like some shipwrecked mariner seeing a companion in misfortune land upon his desert isle.

The poor young priest, still little more than a rather backward boy, had been the prey of some secret despair, though what its nature was she had never really known. So far as she could judge (she took very little interest in such matters) he had believed himself to be a useless soul rejected of God. A species of hatred had taken possession of him, hatred of the loutish, unresponsive countryfolk, to whom he could not talk, whose thoughts were bounded by the land they lived by, who had no need of him. Solitude had sent him nearly mad. Yes, quite literally, he was well on the way to going mad through loneliness. No help had come to him from God. He had told Paula that, as a result of emotional transports and a fleeting visitation of grace, he had believed himself to have a vocation. Once caught in the trap, however, he had never experienced those feelings again. . . . It was as though somebody had laid a baited snare, and then had lost all interest once he was tangled in the net. That, at least, was what Paula had thought he had said. But for her all such concerns belonged to an absurd, an "unthinkable" world. She had listened to his outburst of self-pity with but half an ear, only waiting until he paused for breath to take up the story of her own unhappiness. "And I . . ." she had said, and straight embarked upon the narrative of her marriage. There had been nothing between them but this alternation of monologues. Once only, in the Presbytery garden, and then because he was at the end of his tether, he had, for the space of a few seconds, rested his head upon her shoulder. Almost at once she had slipped away, but not before a neighbor's eye had seen them. That had been the start of the whole business. Because of that single gesture (and it might have changed his whole life) the little lamp was never more to burn before the altar in the family Chapel. The old Baronne had scarcely even protested against the interdict. It was as though she found it natural that the presence of God at Cernès should be thought incompatible with that of the daughter-in-law who had been born a Meulière.

The Weakling and the Enemy

Paula was beginning to feel cold. It was growing dark under the chestnuts. She got up, shook out her skirt, and went back to the path. One of the towers of the great house, dating from the fourteenth century, could be seen from here between the pines. But by now the night was so dark that even this descendant of a race of muleteers could no longer make it out.

For twelve years she had borne upon her back the burden of this calumny, knowing it to be in everybody's mouths. But suddenly the thought that it had reached the ears of a schoolmaster to whom she had never so much as spoken, seemed to her to be beyond all bearing. She knew every man by sight for miles around. There was scarcely one of them she would have failed to recognize at a distance. But the picture of that curly head must have forced its way, almost without her knowledge, into her consciousness—the picture of a schoolmaster whose name was still unknown to her. For schoolmasters and priests have neither of them any need of names. Their function is enough to give them an identity. She could not endure the thought that he should go on believing in this story about her even for one day longer. She would tell him what had really happened. The same imperious need to confess, to lighten herself of a load she could no longer carry, which, twelve years earlier, had led her to confide imprudently in a priest who had been too young and too weak, was nagging at her again. She must fight down her shyness. She must take up the cudgels once again for Guillaume. Perhaps the schoolmaster would yield. In any case, she would have made contact with him. A bond might form between them.

She hung up her cloak in the hall. By force of habit she washed her hands at the scullery sink, then went into the servants' sitting-room, where the family, since the death of Georges, the younger son, had taken to having their meals. The official dining-room, a vast and icy cold apartment, was never used except during the Christmas holidays, and in September, when the Baronne's eldest daughter, the Comtesse d'Arbis, came from Paris with her children and Georges' little daughter, Danièle. On the occasion of those visits, the two garden-boys were put into livery; a cook was engaged; a pair of saddle horses was hired.

This evening, Paula did not go straight to the smaller dining-room. Eager to reopen as soon as possible the argument about the schoolmaster, she made her way instead to her mother-in-law's room. She entered it, perhaps, ten times in the year. She stood now behind the closed door listening to the gay babble of the four conspirators within, to the sound of a tune which Galéas was playing with one finger. Something that Fraülein had just said produced a burst of laughter from the old Baronne. How Paula hated that forced, affected titter! She opened the door without knocking. Like the wooden figures on a public clock those in the room were smitten into sudden immobility. The Baronne sat for a moment with one hand raised, holding a card. Galéas slammed the cover of the piano and swung round on his stool. Fraülein turned toward the enemy, looking for all the world like a cat confronted by a dog, its face flattened in a snarl, its ears laid back, its body arched, and just about to spit. Guillou, surrounded by newspapers from which he had been cutting photographs of airplanes, put his scissors on the table, and curled up once again between the *prie-Dieu* and the bed, drawing in his legs, and playing "possum."

Never before had Paula realized so clearly—accustomed though she was to such scenes—how baleful an influence she exercised on those with whom she had to live. Almost at once, her mother-in-law recovered from the shock of the surprise, and gave her a twisted smile, exhibiting the same slightly excessive amiability that she would have shown to a stranger of inferior social status. She started fussing about the younger woman's damp feet, and told her to come to the fire. Fraülein grumblingly muttered something about its not being worth while because she was just going to serve dinner. She made for the door with Galéas and Guillaume hard at her heels. "As usual," thought the Baronne, "they're unloading her on me."

"Have I your permission, my dear, to put on the fireguard?"

She effaced herself in Paula's presence, and, not for the world would she ever have left a room in front of her daughter-in-law. All the way in to dinner she talked incessantly, making it impossible, until they were all at table, for Paula to get a word in edgeways. Galéas and Guillaume were standing by their chairs. As soon as they were seated, they started noisily lapping their soup. The Baronne asked whether they didn't all think it was very mild today, adding that it was scarcely ever cold at Cernès in November. She had started making her melon jam that very afternoon. This time she was going to try the experiment of mixing it with apricots.

"The sort my poor, dear Adhémar always called, so amusingly, old women's ears—do you remember, Galéas?"

She was talking for the sake of talking. All that mattered

20

was that Paula should not be allowed to start arguing again. But watching her, she saw signs of impending trouble on the hateful face. Guillaume sat with hunched shoulders, uneasy under his mother's watchful eyes. He, too, felt that there was danger in the air, and that it had something to do with him. Try though he might to make himself one with the table and the chair, he knew only too well that Mamie's talk would not fill the silence, and could offer only a feeble barrier to the storm already piling up behind the tight lips of the adversary.

Galéas ate and drank without looking up, bending so low over his food that the graying thicket of hair on the enormous head was at Paula's eye-level. He was hungry, having worked all day in the churchyard, which it was his self-imposed task to keep tidy. Thanks to him there were no neglected graves at Cernès. At the moment he was untroubled, since it was not at him that his wife was looking. He was in luck's way. She had banished him from her mind, which meant that he was the only one of the company who could bask at ease and indulge such whims as pouring wine into his soup, and, as he put it, "trying a little of everything." He mashed and munched, piling his plate with everything on the table, and the Baronne was hard put to it to keep Guillaume from imitating his father without undermining the respect due to him. Papa could do as he liked, she said: but Guillou must sit at table like a well-brought-up little boy. It didn't, in fact, ever occur to him to criticize his father, finding it impossible to imagine him as different from what he was. Papa belonged to a species of grown-ups which threatened no danger. That would have been Guillaume's verdict had he been capable of forming one. Papa never made a noise, never interrupted the stories which Guillaume was forever telling to himself. Indeed, he became part of them, and was no more intrusive than the dogs and oxen on the farm. His mother, on the other hand, broke in upon them with violence, and stuck there like some foreign body. He was not always conscious of her presence, but he knew that she was there. . . . Suddenly, he heard her speak his name. That had torn it!—they were going to talk about him! She mentioned the schoolmaster. He tried to understand what she was saying. He had been dragged by the ears from his earth, and now lay exposed to the glare of the grown-up world.

"But what do you suggest that we should do with Guillaume, then? Have you any alternative to suggest? Oh, I know he can read and write and just about manage to count . . . but that's not saying much for a twelve-year-old. . . ."

According to the Baronne there was no hurry. They must take their time about thinking what would be best to do.

"But he's already been sent away from two schools. You say that this schoolmaster won't do anything about him. In that case, we must have a tutor for him, at home—or a governess."

The old lady protested loudly at such an idea. She would not dream of having a stranger in the house . . . she trembled at the mere thought of exposing their life at Cernès to alien eyes—their life as it had become since the day when Galéas had given his name to this Fury!

"Perhaps *you* can think of something else, my dear?"

Paula emptied her glass at a gulp and refilled it. Both the Baronne and Fraülein had noticed that, since the first year of her marriage, Paula had shown a fondness for the bottle. Fraülein had tried making a pencil mark on the bottles of liqueur so as to check her consumption, but Paula, noticing this, had accumulated in her wardrobe a secret supply of anisette and cherry-brandy, of curaçao and apricot cordial. But this the Austrian woman had discovered. One day, the Baronne had felt it to be her duty to put the dear girl on her guard against strong drink, but her words had led to such an outburst that she had never again dared to refer to the subject.

"In my opinion we have no choice but to try again with the schoolmaster. . . ."

At that, the Baronne raised her hands, declaring that not for any consideration in the world would she expose herself again to the insolence of that Communist. Paula reassured her. There was no question of that, she said. She herself would make the approach, and do her best to succeed where her mother-in-law had failed. She refused to discuss the matter, but said, over and over again, that her mind was quite made up, and that, after all, Guillaume's education was her concern.

"It seems to me that my son might have something to say in the matter!"

"You know that his 'say' will be precisely nothing!"

"If that is how you feel, I have at least the right to insist that you speak to this creature in your own name only. You can, if you like, tell him that I know nothing of your intentions. Should you, however, object to soiling your lips with so white a lie, then I must ask you to make it clear that you are acting contrary to my judgment, and in direct opposition to my wishes."

Paula mockingly suggested that it was the old lady's Christian duty to suffer humiliation for her grandson's sake.

"My dear girl, whatever you have done, or still may do, I

wish it to be fully understood that I am in no way involved. I don't wish to be offensive, but no one could well be less a member of the family than you."

Her tone was perfectly polite, and her long upper lip curled in a smile which revealed her fine and rather too regular teeth.

Paula's nerves were frayed and she found it difficult to contain herself.

"If you wish to imply that I have never shown the slightest wish to resemble the Cernès—you are perfectly right."

"In that case, my dear, there is nothing for you to worry about. No one, I feel sure, has ever done you the wrong of taking you for what you are not."

Guillaume would have liked to slip from the room, but did not dare. Besides, he found this rumbling battle of the gods above his head rather thrilling, though the point of their acid exchanges escaped him.

Galéas got up, leaving the sweets untouched, as he always did when there was cream. The adversaries faced one another.

"It would be a bad day for me if I was to be considered as one of the family when you find the house burning over your head. . . ."

"Are you, by any chance, trying to frighten me? For more than four hundred years the Cernès have always treated their people well, and set a good example. They have been, and are, thank God, loved and respected . . ."

Indignation had set the old voice trembling.

"Loved? . . . Respected? . . . why, you're hated by the whole village. Your obstinacy in keeping Fraülein here during the war. . . ."

"Forgive me for smiling . . . An Austrian of sixty-four, who

24

has lived with us ever since she was a girl! . . . The military authorities thought it wise to shut their eyes—and they were right."

"But the people here are only too glad to have so good an excuse. It is quite incredible that anyone should be so wilfully blind! . . . You have always been detested . . . Do you really think that the tenant-farmers and the tradespeople are taken in by the soft-soap you give them? Because of you, they hate everything you love . . . priests and all. Just you wait and see! . . . Unfortunately, I shall be lumped in with the rest of you. Still, I think I shall die happy!"

She finished by muttering a vulgar phrase which the Baronne had never heard before. "How revealing language can be," thought the old lady, her anger suddenly abated. It sometimes happened that her daughter from Paris, and particularly her grandchildren, would risk using a slang expression in her hearing, but never would they have said anything so common! What, precisely, had it been? "You're going to get it in the neck!"—yes, that was it. As always, Paula's displays of temper had a calming effect on the old lady. She recovered the advantage which self-control always enjoys when at odds with hysteria.

"I would not have you think for a moment that your hatred of the aristocracy surprises me. No matter what may be your opinion, the countryfolk have always loved their masters. Both they and we have a proper self-respect and know our places. It is in the ranks of the lower middle class that you find social hatred, and it springs from envy. It was the middle classes that did most of the butchering during the Terror. . . ."

Her daughter-in-law declared in self-complacent tones that,

owing to the treachery of the emigrés, the Terror had been "just and necessary." At that, the Baronne drew herself majestically to her full height.

"My great-grandfather, and two of my great-uncles perished on the scaffold, and I forbid you . . ."

Paula suddenly found herself thinking of the schoolmaster. Her words would have pleased him. He would have approved her attitude. Paula's views had been inherited from her Meulière uncle, a narrowly fanatical Radical and Free-Mason. But her expression of them took on a special value for her now that she was offering them on the altar of the man she was to see tomorrow. It was a Thursday, and he would be free. What she had said, had been said as a result of *his* influence (uncle Meulière had had nothing to do with it), the influence of someone to whom she had never spoken, whom she had passed occasionally in the street, who never so much as said "Good morning" if she happened to pass when he was working in his garden (though he would pause in his digging to look at her).

"Do you know what you are, my dear?—an incendiary: nothing more nor less than an incendiary. . . ."

Guillaume raised his head. He knew what an incendiary was. Hundreds of times he had looked at a picture in the 1871 volume of *Le Monde Illustré*, which showed two women squatting in the darkness by a cellar door, making some sort of a fire. Locks of untidy hair straggled from underneath their proletarian caps. . . . He gazed at his mother with his mouth open . . . an incendiary?—why, of course she was! . . .

She grabbed him by the arm.

"Upstairs with you—quick now!"

The Weakling and the Enemy

The Baronne made the sign of the cross upon his forehead with her thumb: but she did not kiss him. As soon as he had left the room, she said:

"We ought at least to spare him . . ."

"You needn't worry, he doesn't hear, and if he did hear, he wouldn't understand."

"That is where you are wrong. Poor little mite! He understands a great deal more than we think. . . . And, talking of him brings me back to the subject of our discussion. We seem to have strayed a long way from it, and for that we are equally to blame. If, as I have very little doubt, and, as I hope will be the case, this man persists in his refusal . . ."

"In that case, there'll be nothing for it but to let Guillaume grow up like a little country lout. . . . It's nothing short of a shame to see rich people's children enjoying all the benefits of an education from which they are incapable of profiting, while those of the poor . . ."

Once again, the commonplaces which had been constantly in uncle Meulière's mouth went suddenly to her head. No doubt her views would be shared by the schoolmaster, whom she credited with every kind of advanced theory. It never occurred to her that he might not be built to the official pattern.

The old lady, determined to avoid a fresh outburst, got up without saying a word. Paula followed her to the stairs.

"Why should not you and I join forces and teach him what little we know?"

"If you've got sufficient patience, well and good. I confess that I've had about as much as I can stand."

"A good night's sleep will work wonders, my dear. Please

forget anything I have said that may have wounded you, as I, for my part, freely forgive you."

Her daughter-in-law indulged in a shrug. "That's just so much talk, and doesn't really alter what we feel. We can no longer have any illusions. . . ."

They stood facing one another in the bedroom corridor, candle in hand. Of the two faces thus brightly illuminated, that of the younger woman looked by far the more formidable.

"Please believe, Paula, that I am a great deal less unfair in my attitude toward you than you quite naturally think. You have much to excuse you . . . the burden you have been called upon to bear is heavy for a young woman . . ."

"I was twenty-six," broke in Paula sharply. "I blame nobody. My fate was of my own choosing. If it comes to that, you poor thing . . ."

The meaning behind her words was—my wretched husband is your wretched son. She found some consolation for the hell in which she lived in the knowledge that she shared it with her old enemy. But the Baronne refused the proffered sympathy.

"With me it is quite different," she replied in a voice shaken by emotion. "I, after all, had my Adhémar. For twenty-five years I was the happiest of women. . . ."

"Perhaps . . . but not the happiest of mothers."

"It is five years since my Georges died a hero's death. I do not weep for him. I still have his little Danièle, I still have Galéas. . . ."

"Yes, you most certainly have Galéas!"

"I have my children in Paris," went on the other obstinately.

"But they just sponge on you. For them you have never been

anything but a cow to be milked. You may shake your head as much as you like, but you know it as well as I do. Fraülein throws it in your teeth often enough when the two of you are alone and think that I am out of hearing. . . . No, let me go on . . . I *will* raise my voice if I want to. . . ."

The words, echoing down the corridor, woke Guillaume with a start. He sat up in bed. The gods were still hard at it up there in the sky. He snuggled down again, a pillow pressed against one ear, his finger stuck in the other. While he lay there waiting for sleep to come again, he took up the thread of the story he had been telling himself, about the island and the cave—like in *Un Robinson de Douze Ans*. The night light peopled the linen closet in which he slept with familiar shadows and with monsters tamed.

"We live here deprived of everything so that your Arbis daughter may keep her state in Paris, and weave what she calls her marriage plots. What does it matter if we starve so long as Yolande marries a Duke with Jewish blood, and Stanislas an American nobody. . . ."

Thus did Paula nag away at the old lady who, eager for silence, retreated hurriedly and bolted her door. But through the panels the implacable voice still sounded.

"The fewer hopes you have of Stanislas, the better. *He'll* never marry anybody, that little . . ."

She finished up with a word the meaning of which the Baronne would not have grasped even if she had heard it, even if she had not been kneeling at her *prie-Dieu* with her head buried in her arms.

No sooner had Paula shut herself into her own room than her anger fell dead. There were still a few embers glowing in the grate. She threw on a fresh log, lit the oil lamp on the table by the sofa, undressed in front of the fire, and put on an old quilted dressing gown.

We speak of "making love": we should be able, too, to speak of "making hate." To make hate is comforting. It rests the mind and relaxes the nerves. Paula opened the wardrobe. Her hands hovered, momentarily hesitating. Then she chose the curaçao, pitched the sofa cushions onto the floor, as near the fire as possible, and stretched herself out at full length with a glass and a bottle within easy reach of her hand. She started to smoke and to drink, thinking the while of the man, of the schoolmaster, who was the enemy of all aristocrats and rich folk, a "red," maybe, a Communist. He was despised as she was despised, and by the same type of person. Before him she would humble herself, and, in the end, would force her way into his life. He was married . . . what was his wife like? She did not even know her by sight. For the time being she kept her strictly out of the story she was imagining, burrowing into her fantasy, prodigal of more invention than ever professional story-teller showed. Before her inner eye visions arose beyond the power of language to express. Now and again she got to her feet to put another log upon the fire and fill her glass. Then she lay down again. The occasional flicker of a flame played on her face, revealing alternately the mask of a criminal—or of a martyr.

2

EARLY next afternoon, wearing a mackintosh, heavy shoes, and a beret pulled down over her eyes, she made her way to the village. The rain beating on her face, she thought, would wash away the telltale signs of last night's orgy. She no longer felt exalted. Only determination kept her going. Any other woman would have spent hours choosing what clothes she should put on for so important a mission, or, if not that, would at least have tried to look her best. It never so much as occurred to Paula to powder her face, or to do anything that would make the hirsute appearance of her cheeks less noticeable. If only she had washed her hair it might have looked less greasy. It should have entered her mind that the schoolmaster might, like most other men, be susceptible to scent. . . . But no: without paying any more attention than usual to her person, and looking as bedraggled as always, she set out to try her luck for the last time.

The man, the schoolmaster, was sitting in the kitchen, facing his wife. He was shelling kidney-beans, and chatting as he worked. . . . It was Thursday, the best day of the whole week. The schoolhouse faced the street, like all the other houses of the ugly village of Cernès. The smithy, the butcher's shop, the Inn, and the post office were not, as elsewhere, grouped about the Church, which, set in solitude among its huddle of graves, stood upon a promontory, dominating the valley of the Ciron. . . . Cernès had only one street, and even that was not a street proper, but only the main road. The schoolhouse stood a little way back from it. The children used the front door, and the schoolmaster's kitchen opened off to the right of the narrow passage which led to the playground, and, beyond it, to the kitchen-garden. Robert and Léone Bordas, untouched by any presentiment of the fate which was approaching their home, were once again hard at it, discussing their strange visitor of the day before.

"It's all very well your talking," his wife was saying with no little eagerness, "but a hundred and fifty, perhaps two hundred francs extra each month, just for seeing that the kid from the great house keeps his nose to the grindstone, are not to be sneezed at. Anyway, it's worth thinking about."

"We haven't sunk that far. There's nothing, so far as I can see, that we have to do without. I'm getting practically all the books I want now. . . ." (he did the reviewing of poetry and fiction for the *Teachers' Journal*).

"You never think about anybody but yourself. After all, there's Jean-Pierre to be considered. . . ."

"Jean-Pierre's got all he needs. You're not suggesting, I suppose, that he should have a coach?"

Her smile expressed satisfaction. No, certainly, their boy didn't need anything of that kind. He was always top of his class in every subject. Though he was only thirteen, he had just got into the upper school a good two years ahead of the normal time, and would almost certainly have to stay in it an extra three terms, because it was very unlikely that his age would be taken into account. He was already being picked for a winner at the Lycée, and his masters had very little doubt that he would pass the school certificate at the first attempt, both in science and the humanities.

"That's where you're wrong: I do want him to take private lessons."

As Léone made this announcement there was nothing in the expression of her face to indicate either that she had any doubts of her own wisdom, or that she felt she was asking a favor. She was a thin, pale woman with reddish hair and small features. Though not in her first youth, she was still pretty. Her voice was rather sharp and penetrating as a result of having to keep a roomful of youngsters in order.

"He must learn riding."

Robert Bordas went on with his task of shelling beans. He affected to believe that she was joking.

"Of course he must, and dancing too, I suppose, if you want him to."

Laughter creased his long and rather narrow eyes. He was wearing no collar and was unshaven. Nevertheless, there was something still of the charm of youth about him. It was easy to see what he must have been like as a boy. He got up and moved round the table, leaning on a cane with a rubber ferrule. He limped, but only very little. His long, supple cat's back was that of an adolescent. He lit a cigarette and said:

"I know somebody who longs for the Revolution—but wants a racing-stable for her son!"

She shrugged her shoulders.

"Why do you want to turn Jean-Pierre into a horseman"— he would not let the subject drop—"So he can serve in the

Dragoons with a lot of rotters who'll send the schoolmaster's son to Coventry?"

"Don't get excited. You'd better take care of your voice. You'll need it at the November 11th Meeting. . . ."

She saw from his face that she had gone too far, emptied her apronful of beans into a dish, and gave her husband a kiss. "Listen to me, Robert. . . ." She wanted the same things that he wanted. He knew that. She followed him blindly and with utter confidence. Politics were not for her. She found it difficult to imagine how the world would go once the Revolution was an accomplished fact. The only thing she knew for certain was that there would always be an élite who would rule the country. It would be drawn, of course, from the most intelligent and the best educated, but also from those with the gift of leadership.

"All right then, I do want Jean-Pierre to know how to ride a horse, and, more than anything, I want him to acquire those virtues of initiative, courage and enterprise in which he is rather lacking. He's got everything else, but not them."

Robert Bordas looked at the absent expression on his wife's face. She was completely unaware of him. Her heart, at that moment, was far away.

"The Ecole Normale trains an élite of University teachers," he observed with a touch of dryness. "That is the sole purpose of its existence."

"But think of all the Ministers, all the great writers, all the Party chiefs, who have passed through it: Jaurès, first and foremost, Léon Blum . . ."

He broke in on her. "Personally speaking, I should be quite proud enough if Jean-Pierre could produce a first-rate thesis, and end up as a Professor in the Faculty of Letters. I ask nothing better for him . . . or even, perhaps, at the Sorbonne, or, who knows . . . at the Collège de France!"

There was a touch of bitterness in her laughter.

"It's my turn now to point out what a fine revolutionary *you* make! Do you really imagine that all those antiques will be left standing?"

"Of course they will! The University will be transformed, no doubt, and injected with new blood. But in France, higher education will always be higher education . . . You don't know what you're talking about. . . ."

Suddenly he stopped speaking. He had just seen, through the glazed panel of the door, the figure of a woman emerging from the mist.

"Who on earth is that?"

"Some mother, I expect, who has come to complain that her darling is being treated unfairly."

Paula took a long time scraping her shoes and ridding them of mud before she entered the house. They did not recognize her. They had no idea who this strange woman could be, with a beret pulled down over dark, black-circled eyes, and a face which had as thick a growth of down as a youth's. She carefully avoided mentioning her name. All she said to Robert was that she was the mother of the boy about whom the Baronne de Cernès had spoken to him on the previous day. It took him a few seconds to grasp the significance of her words, but Léone had already guessed.

She led the way into a freezingly cold room and threw open the shutters. Everything was bright and shining, the floor, the sideboard and the table in department-store style. A coarse lace blind masked the window. There was a wide frieze with a design of giant hydrangeas just below the ceiling. The wallpaper was dark red.

"I will leave you with my husband. . . ."

Paula protested that she had no secrets to discuss. It was just a question of clearing up a slight misunderstanding. Robert Bordas' cheeks had flushed a bright red. They had always done that ever since he was a child. His ears were aflame. Was this woman with the evil gleam in her eye going to make him give an account of his yesterday's half-joking behavior? Indeed she was! She had the brazen effrontery to embark at once on the subject, without the slightest show of embarrassment. She was afraid, she said, that her mother-in-law had misunderstood some perfectly innocent remark of his, and had gone off in a huff. She had no intention of asking Monsieur Bordas to withdraw his refusal, but she would hate to think that the incident had created a new enemy for herself in the village. She was so defenseless, and he was one of the few persons from whom she had the right to expect some measure of understanding.

She turned her blazing eyes from Robert to Léone. The slightly drooping corners of her mouth gave the look of a tragic mask to the great hairy face. Robert stammered that he was deeply shocked, that there had been no intention of offense in what he had said. Paula cut him short, and, turning to Léone:

"I never thought there had been," she said. "You have only too good reason to know, both of you, what the people round here are like, and how they gossip."

Had they understood the veiled allusion? Had they heard

the story which was going round to the effect that the school-master had been wounded while holding a cushy job in one of the back-areas? Some went so far as to hint that he had let off his own rifle . . . pure clumsiness, of course, but . . .

They showed no sign of embarrassment. Paula had no idea whether she had touched them on the raw or not.

She went on: "I know, madame, that you come of an old Cadillac family . . ."

It was, indeed, true that Léone's parents were peasant-proprietors in a small way, and belonged to an honorable and ancient line. But they had been looked at askance because of their advanced views. Their daughter had not had a church wedding, and there seemed to be some doubt as to whether Jean-Pierre had been baptized. In order to stay near the family, the Bordas' had given up a chance of rapid promotion.

"Cernès," said Paula, "has a better schoolmaster than it deserves."

Once again the young face opposite flushed crimson. But there was no stopping her. She knew, she said, that Robert Bordas had only to raise a finger to be a Deputy tomorrow if he chose. His color deepened, but he merely shrugged his shoulders: "You're pulling my leg!" Léone laughed: "You'll be turning my poor Robert's head, madame!"

The young man's face creased in a smile.

"I'm not expressing my own views. It was Monsieur Lousteau, our bailiff, who said that. He's a friend of yours, I believe? Of course, he's a Royalist, but he can be fair to his enemies. With a husband like yours, madame, a woman can afford to be ambitious."

In a low voice, she added: "If I were in your shoes! . . ." The tone in which she said this was exactly right. There was no undue stressing of the allusion to her own wretched husband.

"Jean-Pierre will be the first great man in *our* family," said the schoolmaster with a laugh, "isn't that so, Léone?"

Their son? The visitor's smile expressed understanding. His fame had reached even her ears. Monsieur Lousteau had often spoken of him. How happy they must be, and how proud! Again she sighed, again she showed that her own misfortune was uppermost in her mind. But this time she made no bones about talking of it.

"Speaking of infant prodigies reminds me. It was to discuss the future of my own son that I came here today. I think it not unlikely that my mother-in-law may have slightly exaggerated the position. He *is* backward, I know, and I realize that the suggestion she made may rather have frightened you!"

Robert protested vigorously that lack of leisure, and the dread of not being able to devote enough time to an additional job, had alone prompted his refusal. His duties as Mayor's secretary, and his own private work, took up every moment he could spare from his teaching.

"Oh, I know what a worker you are!" she said, adding in a sly tone of flattery: "a little bird has been whispering that certain unsigned articles in *la France du Sud-Ouest* . . ."

Once again, the schoolmaster's cheeks and ears glowed scarlet. In order to cut the interview short, he began to put a few questions to her about Guillaume. Could the boy read and write fluently? He actually read sometimes for pleasure, did he?— well, then, he certainly was not a hopeless case.

Paula felt a little uncertain how to proceed. It was important not to put this man off at the start. All the same, it was only wise to make him realize what a little half-wit his future pupil was. Yes, she said, there were two or three books which he read over and over again, and he was forever browsing over bound numbers of the *Saint-Nicholas Annual* dating from the 'nineties, though there was no reason to think that he took anything in. She was afraid her little brat was not very attractive, not very winning. One had to be his mother before one could put up with him at all, and there were times when even she . . . The schoolmaster felt his heart bleed for her. The best thing, he suggested, would be for him to have the boy round after five o'clock one evening, when school was over, just to see what he was like. He would not make any definite promise until he had had an opportunity to study him.

Paula took both his hands in hers. Emotion, only half feigned, made her voice tremble as she said: "I can't help thinking of the difference you will find between my poor, unhappy boy and your own son!"

She turned away her face as though to keep him from seeing how ashamed she felt. . . . Her behavior, this afternoon, had been nothing short of inspired! Something undreamed of had happened to this teacher and his schoolmarm wife. They had grown used to living in an atmosphere of perpetual hostility, of being objects of suspicion to countryfolk and gentry alike, of being treated by the clergy as public enemies—and now, someone from the great house had come to ask a favor of them! Just fancy what it must mean to them to know that she not only admired, but actually envied, them! In how humble a tone had she referred to her own husband and her degenerate son! . . . The adventure had quite gone to Robert's head. He could not

39

forget that this beret and this mackintosh concealed a genuine lady of title! He could not resist a little mild badinage.

"I find it a little surprising, madame, that you should not be afraid of my influence on the boy. . . . My views, you know, are not at all what is usually called respectable."

Again the creases appeared in his face. His eyes almost vanished, so that only their glitter showed between the half-closed lids.

"You don't know me," replied Paula with a serious air—"or what I am really like."

If she told them that nothing would please her more than to think her poor boy capable of feeling that influence, they would not believe her.

"The world in which I live is not my world. I am just as much a fish out of water as you would be . . . one of these days I'll tell you . . ."

In this way did she prepare the way for future confidences. No need to say more: no need to break down barriers. She would say good-bye now, for the time being, leaving them quite overwhelmed by what she had just said about her "views." . . . It was agreed that she should bring Guillaume to the schoolhouse next afternoon, about four. Then, all of a sudden, she became the great lady, the replica of her mother-in-law, of the Comtesse d'Arbis.

"So many thanks! You have no idea how relieved I feel. Yes, really, I mean it. Our little chat has meant *so* much to me."

"It's pretty obvious she's fallen for you," said Léone.

She had cleared the table, and now, with a sigh, took up a number of exercises which she had to correct.

"She's not a bad sort, you know."

"There you are! She was very careful to treat you with respect, but, if you want my opinion, you'd better watch your step!"

"She's a bit touched, I should say . . . or, to put it mildly, rather hysterical."

"She knows what she wants all right, touched or not. Don't forget that story about her and the curé! I think you ought to go very carefully."

He got up, stretched his long arms, and said: "I don't like bearded ladies."

"She wouldn't be bad looking," said Léone, "if she took more care of herself."

"I remember now what Lousteau told me. She's not an aristocrat by birth, but the daughter, or niece, of Meulière who was once Mayor of Bordeaux. . . . Why are you laughing?"

"Her not being a genuine aristocrat seems to depress you!"

While his mother was making ready to hand him over to the tender mercies of the red schoolmaster, the poor little hare, hunted from his form, was wondering whether he would ever get back to it. The bright light of the grown-up world into which he had been chased made him blink. During his mother's absence, a difference of opinion had developed between his three beneficent deities—papa, Mamie and Fräulein. Mamie and Fräulein, it is true, were frequently at loggerheads, but almost always about things which didn't much matter. The Austrian woman would sometimes employ language which seemed the cruder for being couched in the respectful third person. But today Guillaume had an uncomfortable feeling that even Fräulein was in favor of his being entrusted to the schoolmaster.

"Why should he not have a proper education? He's as good as anybody else!"

Then, turning to him: "Run away and play, my duckie, my chickabiddy. . . ."

He left the house, but, a moment later, came back and slipped into the kitchen. Wasn't it the general view that he never listened, and that, even if he did, he couldn't understand?

The Baronne, without condescending to answer Fraülein, was haranguing her son, who was lolling in his favorite wicker armchair in front of the kitchen fire. He spent almost every rainy afternoon there, making paper spills, or polishing his father's guns, which he never used.

"Do exert a little authority, for once in your life, Galéas!" the old lady was saying. "You've only got to say, 'No, I won't have my son handed over to this Communist!' . . . There'll be a storm, of course, but it'll blow over."

Fraülein entered a protest: "Don't you listen to Madame la Baronne. Why should not Guillou be as well educated as the Arbis children?"

"You leave the Arbis children alone, Fraülein. This has got nothing to do with them. I don't wish my grandson to be inculcated with this man's ideas—that's the long and the short of it."

"Poor chick! As though anyone was going to talk politics to him!"

"It is not a question of politics. . . . There is religion to be considered. The boy's not so strong in his catechism as he might be. . . ."

Guillaume watched his father sitting there without stirring a finger. He was staring at the smoldering logs, and showed no sign of inclining to one side or other of the argument. Guillou, his mouth half open, was trying hard to understand.

"Madame la Baronne does not really mind him living like a clodhopper when he's grown up . . . for all I know, she may prefer to have it that way!"

"The idea of you setting yourself up against me and pleading my grandson's cause! That really is too much!" The Baronne tried to sound indignant, but it was clear that she did not feel very sure of herself.

"Oh, I know that Madame la Baronne is very fond of Guillou, and likes having him with her here; but it is not him she has in mind when she thinks about the future of the family."

The Baronne professed to regard Fraülein as a bull in a china shop. But the Austrian's shrill voice easily drowned her mistress's.

"And the proof of that, if proof were needed, is that after Georges' death, it was agreed that Stanislas, the eldest Arbis boy, should add the name Cernès to his own, as though there were no other Cernès left, as though Guillou wasn't really Guillaume de Cernès."

"The boy's listening," said Galéas suddenly, and then relapsed once more into silence. Fraülein took Guillou by the shoulders and gently pushed him through the door. But he went no further than the pantry, where Fraülein's loud tones reached him easily.

"I know somebody who wasn't called 'Desiré' when he turned up. Madame la Baronne will doubtless remember her own words—that it couldn't be a very common occurrence for an invalid to get a child on his sicknurse. . . ."

The Weakling and the Enemy

"I never said any such thing, Fraülein! . . . Galéas was perfectly well and strong. . . . Besides, it is not my custom to make coarse remarks of that kind."

"Madame la Baronne will surely recollect that a child was no part of the bargain. I, who knew my Galéas, was well aware that he was as good as the next man—as the event proved. . . ."

A dangerous glitter showed between the Austrian's reddish, lashless lids—"pig's eyes"—Madame Galéas had once called them. The Baronne, shocked by what had just been said, turned away.

Guillaume, his nose pressed to the pantry window, was watching the splashing raindrops. They looked like little dancing figures. The grown-ups seemed to be forever going on about him, and quarrelling, too. No one had found it possible to call him "Desiré." He wanted to go on telling himself the stories which only he knew. But this time there would be no excuse, unless the schoolmaster went on refusing. If he did that, Guillou would be so happy that he wouldn't a bit mind not being called "Desiré." All he asked was not to have to be with a lot of other children who would make his life a misery to him, not to have anything to do with schoolmasters with their loud voices, their bad temper, their stern looks, and the way they had of producing a lot of words which didn't mean anything.

Mamie hadn't wanted him, nor his own mother either. He knew that all right. Had they foreseen that he wouldn't be like other boys? How about poor papa?—had *he* wanted him? He didn't know, but he did know that papa wouldn't be any good at getting him out of the schoolmaster's clutches.

The Baronne was keeping on at that very subject, until she was sick of the sound of her own voice.

"You've only got to say 'no'—surely it's not all that difficult! Listen to me, it's just a question of saying 'no' . . . Since you've only got to say 'no' . . ."

But all he did was to sit there shaking his great mop of grizzled hair, and saying nothing. Finally, however, he did speak:

"I haven't the right . . ."

"Haven't the right? What do you mean, Galéas? Who, then, has a right if not the father of a family, where his children's education is concerned?"

But he kept on shaking his head, looking mulish, and repeating:

"I haven't the right . . ."

It was then that Guillaume ran back into the room in tears, and flung himself into Fraülein's lap.

"Here's mummy!—and she's laughing to herself. Oh! I know it means that the schoolmaster's going to . . ."

"What of it, you little silly? He won't eat you! Wipe his nose, Fraülein, he's a disgusting sight."

He vanished into the scullery, just as his mother entered the kitchen with a look of triumph on her face.

"It's all arranged," she said. "I'm to take Guillaume along there tomorrow afternoon at four."

"If your husband is agreeable."

"Oh naturally; but he'll be agreeable all right, won't you, Galéas?"

"You're going to have your work cut out with that boy, whatever you do. . . ."

"That reminds me—where is he?" asked Paula. "I thought I heard him snuffling."

They caught sight of Guillaume sneaking out of the scullery.

45

He was looking his very worst, with tears and dribble and snot all over his face.

"I won't go!" he whined, without looking at his mother. "I won't go to the schoolmaster!"

Paula had always been ashamed of him, but now, behind the boy's puckered face was the image of the father in his chair. The child's drooling mouth was the very replica of that other mouth, moist, and without warmth.

With an effort she controlled her temper. In a voice that was almost gentle she said: "Of course, I can't drag you there by force. But, if you won't go, you'll have to be sent away to board at the Lycée."

The Baronne shrugged her shoulders. "You know perfectly well that no school would keep such a little misery."

"Then I see nothing for it but a Reformatory . . ."

She had uttered this particular threat so often that Guillaume had ended by conjuring up a vague but terrifying image of those disciplinary establishments. He began to tremble. "No! mummy, no!" he blubbered, and, hurling himself into Fraülein's arms, hid his face against her flabby bosom.

"Don't you believe a word she says, my chick. You don't think I'd let her do a thing like that, do you?"

"Fraülein has no say in the matter. And this time I'm not joking. I have made inquiries, and have several addresses," said Paula, and there was a note of gay excitement in her voice.

What finally brought him to the breaking point was the sound of old Mamie's laughter.

"Why not just put him in a sack, my dear, and have done with it? Why not throw him into the river like a kitten?"

The Weakling and the Enemy

Mad with terror, he began scrubbing away at his face with a filthy handkerchief.

"Oh, no, Mamie, no!—not in a sack!" Irony meant nothing to him. Everything he heard he took quite literally.

"Little silly!" said the Baronne, and drew him to her, but only to push him away again, quite gently.

"Really, it is difficult to know what to do for the best. Such a grubby little urchin—take him, Fraülein . . . run away, my boy, and clean yourself."

His teeth were chattering. "I *will* go to the schoolmaster, mummy; I *will* be good! . . ."

"Ah, now you're seeing sense at last!"

Fraülein took him along to the scullery and washed his face at the tap.

"They only want to frighten you, my chick. They don't mean what they say; just you laugh at them!"

At this point Galéas got out of his chair, and, without a glance at any of them, said:

"It's quite fine now. You coming along to the churchyard, son?"

Guillou dreaded going for walks with his father, but this time, he gladly took the proffered hand, and started off, still snuffling.

It had stopped raining, and the drenched grass was sparkling in the warm sunlight. They walked along a field-path which skirted the village. Ordinarily, Guillaume was afraid of cows, of the way they raised their heads and stared, as though they were making up their minds to charge. His father had tight hold of his hand, and said nothing. They could have walked for hours without exchanging a word. Guillou could not know that these long silences were his father's despair, that the poor man was trying, all the while, to concentrate his mind. But he could not think of anything to say to a small boy.

They entered the churchyard through a hole in the wall, choked with nettles. It lay at the east end of the building.

The graves were still covered with the faded remnants of flowers laid there on All Saints' Day. Galéas dropped his son's hand, and went in search of a barrow. Guillou watched him walk away. That was his father—that darned brown jersey, those trouser legs which looked as though there were nothing inside them, that tousled head under the tiny beret. He waited for him, seated on a gravestone which was half buried in the grass. The late sun had warmed it slightly. All the same, he felt cold. The thought came to him that he might catch a chill, that he might not be able to leave the house tomorrow. To die . . . to become like the people he tried to imagine lying under this rich soil—the dead, those human moles, marking their presence with little heaps of earth.

Beyond the wall he could see the countryside already emptied of life by the approach of winter: the shivering vines, the greasy, sticky soil—the elements at odds with man, to which it would be as mad to trust oneself as to the waves of the sea. At the bottom of the slope the Ciron flowed on toward the river, a small stream, swollen by the rains, moving through mysterious marshlands and a tangled wilderness of water plants. Guillou had heard the villagers say that sometimes they had put up woodcook there. Like one of them, the boy, driven from his hiding-place, sat trembling with cold and fear, with nothing to protect him from a hostile world and nature's cruelty. On the hillside, the industrial red of brand-new roofs shone harshly. Instinctively, his eyes sought the rain-worn pink of old and round-backed tiles. Close at hand, the church wall showed dishonorable cracks. One of the colored windows had been broken. He knew that "the Good God was not there," that the curé would not leave God in such a place for fear of sacrilege. Nor was the Good God in their Chapel at home, which Fraülein used now as a room in which to keep brooms and packing-cases and broken chairs. Where in this harsh world had God set up His dwelling? Where was a trace of Him to be found?

Guillou felt cold. A nettle had stung him on the calf. He got up and walked the few paces which lay between him and the War Memorial, unveiled the year before. There were thirteen names for this one small village: De Cernès, Georges; Laclotte, Jean; Lapeyre, Joseph; Lapeyre, Ernest; Lartigue, René. . . . Guillaume saw between the gravestones his father's brown jersey bend down, then straighten, and heard the squeaking of the barrow wheels. Tomorrow he was to be handed over to the red schoolmaster. Perhaps the schoolmaster would die suddenly in the night. Something might happen—a hurricane, an earthquake . . . But nothing would ever silence his mother's terrible voice, nothing would ever put out the terrible gleam in her eyes which, when they rested on him, made him conscious, all at once, of his skinniness, of his dirty knees, of his wrinkled and untidy socks. On those occasions, Guillaume would swallow his saliva, and, in the hope of pacifying the enemy, shut his mouth. . . . But the exasperated voice shattered the silence (it was as though it had pursued him into the tiny graveyard where he stood shivering). "Oh, go away, do; anywhere you like, so long as I don't see you!"

49

The Weakling and the Enemy

About the same time, Paula had lit the fire in her bedroom, and was giving free play to her thoughts. No one can make themselves beloved at will, or attract another merely by wishing to. But no power in Heaven, or in the earth beneath can keep a woman from picking out one man from the crowd, and choosing him to be her god. It does not matter to him, since he is not asked to give anything in return. It is she who decides to make him the idol at the center of her life. There is nothing she can do but raise an altar in the desert, and consecrate it to her curly-headed divinity.

Others, in the end, always ask favors of their god, but she was determined to ask nothing of hers. She would rob him only of what can be taken from another without his knowledge. . . . How miraculous a power dwells in the furtive glance, in the undisciplined thought! A day might come perhaps when she would dare to make some gesture of approach, and then— who knows?—her god might bear, without flinching, the touch of lips upon his hand.

3

HURRIEDLY, his mother dragged him along the road. The ruts were filled with rain-water. They passed the children going home from school, who spoke no word, nor laughed. The satchels on their backs were only to be guessed at from the way they showed as humps beneath the capes. Dark eyes and light from all these little hunchbacks gleamed from the shadow of their hoods. Guillou thought how soon they would have grown to be tormentors had he been forced to work and play with them. But he was to be delivered, sole and unaccompanied, to the schoolmaster who would have no one else to occupy his mind, who would concentrate upon his single person that terrifying power all grown-ups had to crush him with their questions, to weigh upon him with their arguments and explanations. No longer would that power be spread over a whole classroom of children. Guillou, and Guillou alone, would have to stand up to this monster of knowledge, who would be exasperated, irritated, by the presence of a boy who could not even understand the words with which his ears were being deafened.

He was going to school at a time when the other pupils were on their way home. The thought that that was so made a deep impression on him. He felt different, he felt lonely. The dry, warm hand which held his own tightened its grip. A force that

was indifferent, if not actually hostile, to his feelings, was drag-
ging him along. Shut away in a secret world of passions and
of thoughts, his mother spoke not a single word. Already they
had reached the first houses of the village. The lamps and the
firelight shining behind the clouded window panes, cast a
radiance on the dusk. The smoke of chimneys filled the night
air with a smell of burning. From the Hotel Dupuy there
streamed a brighter glow. Two wagons were standing in
front of the door. The broad backs of their drivers were jos-
tling before the bar. Still a minute to go. The light over there
—*that* was it. He remembered the gruff voice his grandmother
put on when she told him the tale of *Tom Thumb*—*"It was
the ogre's house!"* Through the glass panes of the front door
he could see the ogre's wife on the lookout for her prey.

"What are you trembling for, you little fool? Monsieur
Bordas won't eat you."

"Perhaps he's cold?"

Paula shrugged and said irritably: "No, it's just nerves. It
always takes him like that, for no apparent reason. He suffered from convulsions when he was eighteen months old."

Guillou's teeth were chattering. The only sound to be heard
was the noise they made, and the ticking of the grandfather
clock.

"Take off his boots, Léone," said the ogre, "and give him
Jean-Pierre's slippers."

"Oh, please," protested Paula, "don't go to all that trouble."

But already Léone was coming back into the room with a
pair of slippers. She perched Guillou on her knee, took off his
cape, and moved close to the fire.

The Weakling and the Enemy

"Aren't you ashamed, a great big boy like you?" said his mother. "I haven't brought any of his schoolbooks or notebooks with me," she added.

The ogre assured her that he did not need them. This evening they would just talk and get to know each other.

"I'll come back in two hours," said Paula. Guillou could not hear what his mother and the schoolmaster were whispering in the entry. He knew that she had gone because he no longer felt cold. The front door had been shut.

"Would you like to help us shell kidney-beans?" Léone asked. "But perhaps you don't know how?"

He laughed and said that he always helped Fraülein. This talk of beans gave him a sense of security. He plucked up courage to add:

"Ours have been picked for a long time."

"These," said the schoolmaster's wife, "are the late kind. A lot of them are bad; you'll have to sort them out."

Guillou drew up to the table and started on the work. The Bordas' kitchen was like every other kitchen. It had a wide hearth with a pot hanging from a hook, a long table, copper saucepans on a dresser, a row of jam jars on another, and two hams in sacks suspended from the beams. . . . But Guillou felt that he had come into a strange, delicious world. Was it the smell of the pipe which was always in Monsieur Bordas' mouth, even when it wasn't alight? What most struck him were the books everywhere, and the piles of magazines on the sideboard and on a small table which stood within easy reach of the schoolmaster's hand. He sat there now, with his legs stretched out, paying no attention to Guillou, but engaged in cutting the pages of a Review which had a white cover with the title printed in red.

Above the chimney-piece was the portrait of a big, bearded man with folded arms. There was a word printed beneath it which the boy tried to spell out in a low voice from where he was sitting: "Jaur . . . Jaur. . . ."

"Jaurès," said the ogre suddenly. "Do you know who Jaurès was?"

Guillou shook his head. Léone broke in: "Surely you're not going to start by talking to him about Jaurès?"

"He began it," said Monsieur Bordas. He laughed. Guillou liked his eyes when they were all squinnied up with laughter. He would have liked to know who Jaurès was. He didn't at all mind shelling kidney-beans. He made a separate pile of the bad ones. He was being left to himself. He could think his own thoughts and take in the ogre, the ogre's wife and their house.

"Had enough of it?" Monsieur Bordas asked suddenly.

He was not reading his Review. He glanced through the table of contents, cut the pages, paused now and again at the names of the various contributors, held the paper close to his face, sniffing at it greedily. A magazine straight from Paris. He thought how unbelievably happy must be the lives of the men who worked on it. He tried to picture their faces, the editor's room where they met to exchange views . . . men, all of them, who knew everything, who had made the "circuit of the human mind." . . . Léone did not know that he had sent in an essay he had written on Romain Rolland. It had been refused, though the letter that told him so had been extremely polite. His approach had been too markedly political.

The Weakling and the Enemy

The rain was now splashing on the roof and gurgling in the gutters. One has only one life, and Robert Bordas would never know what it was like to live in Paris. Monsieur Lousteau was forever telling him that he could write a book about his experiences at Cernès, and advising him to keep a Journal. But he wasn't interested in himself. He wasn't, if it came to that, very much interested in other people either. He would have liked to persuade them, impose his ideas on them, but as individuals they did not appeal to him. . . . He had the gift of words, of writing articles at short notice. Monsieur Lousteau thought his contributions to *la France du Sud-Ouest* better than anything published in Paris, except in *l'Action française*. There was no one on the staff of *l'Humanité,* so Lousteau said, to hold a candle to him. . . . Paris . . . He had promised Léone never to leave Cernès, not even when Jean-Pierre went to the Ecole Normale . . . not even later, when their son should have made his mark and was occupying a high position. He mustn't be an old man of the sea, mustn't get in the lad's way. "Everyone's got his own place in life," said Léone. Robert got up and stood for a while with his face pressed to the glass panel of the front door. Coming back into the room, he saw Guillou's moist and gentle eyes fixed upon him. The boy looked away as he approached, and the schoolmaster remembered that he liked reading.

"Had enough of shelling beans, old man? Like me to lend you a picture-book?"

Guillou replied that it wouldn't matter if there weren't any pictures.

"Show him Jean-Pierre's library," said Léone, "then he can choose for himself."

55

The Weakling and the Enemy

Monsieur Bordas, carrying a paraffin lamp, led the way into the family bedroom. To the boy, following him, it seemed magnificent. The huge carved bedstead was dominated by a cherry-colored eiderdown. It was as though red-currant syrup had been spilled all over the counterpane. A number of enlarged photographs hung on the walls, close to the ceiling. Monsieur Bordas introduced him into a smaller room which had a slightly stuffy smell. It seemed to have been shut up for some time. The schoolmaster proudly raised the lamp, and, at once, Guillou was lost in admiration of Bordas Junior's room.

"Not so fine as up at the big house, of course," said his guide. "Still," he added, with a self-satisfied air, "it's not too bad. . . ."

The boy could scarcely believe his eyes. For the first time this little scion of a noble line found himself thinking of the hole in which he spent his nights. It was impregnated with the smell of Mademoiselle Adrienne who was in charge of the household linen, and spent all her afternoons there. A dressmaker's dummy, now out of use, stood beside a sewing machine, and there was a truckle bed covered with a dustsheet, which Fraülein occupied when Guillou was ill. He had a sudden vision of the shabby piece of rug on which he had so often upset his chamber pot. This room was all Jean-Pierre's own, with its painted bed in blue and white, and its glass-fronted, well-stocked bookcase.

"Almost all the volumes are prizes," said Monsieur Bordas. "He's always top of his form."

Guillou touched each separate book with loving fingers.

"Take what you'd like."

"Oh! . . . *The Mysterious Island!* . . . have you read that?"

56

he asked, looking at Monsieur Bordas with shining eyes.

"Yes, I read it when I was your age," said the schoolmaster, "but, d'you know, I've forgotten every word . . . it's a sort of Robinson Crusoe story, isn't it?"

"It's ever so much better than Robinson Crusoe!" said Guillou with enthusiasm.

"In what way is it better?"

This direct question sent the boy back into his shell. The vague, almost vacant, look reappeared on his face.

"I always thought it was a sequel to something else," went on Monsieur Bordas, after a pause.

"It is. You ought to have read *Twenty Thousand Leagues Under the Sea,* first, and *Captain Grant's Children.* . . . I haven't read *Twenty Thousand Leagues Under the Sea,* but it doesn't really make any difference. You can understand *The Mysterious Island* just the same . . . except where Cyrus Smith makes things like dynamite . . . I always skip those parts."

"Isn't there a shipwrecked man on one of the neighboring islands whom the engineer's companions discover?"

"Yes, he's called Ayrton, you know. There's a lovely bit when Cyrus Smith says to him, 'If you can cry that means you are a man.'"

Without looking at the boy, Monsieur Bordas took the fat, red-bound book and held it out.

"Try and find the place . . . I seem to remember; there's a picture, I think."

"It's at the end of chapter fifteen," said Guillou.

"Read that page to me . . . it'll take me back to my childhood."

The Weakling and the Enemy

He lit an oil lamp and settled Guillou at a table covered with Jean-Pierre's ink-stains. The boy began to read in a muffled voice. At first the schoolmaster could catch only one or two words. He was sitting far back in the shadows, scarcely daring to breathe. It was as though he were afraid of startling a wild bird. Gradually, the reader's voice grew stronger and more distinct. He had forgotten now that anyone was listening.

". . . When they reached the spot where the first tall trees of the forest grew, their leaves faintly stirring in the breeze, the stranger began greedily sniffing the smell which filled the air. He sighed deeply. The planters kept well behind, ready to seize him should he make any attempt to escape. And indeed, the poor wretch was about to plunge into the creek which lay between him and the forest. For a brief moment his legs were like two springs at the moment of release. . . . But almost at once he fell back, half collapsing, and a large tear welled up in his eye. 'Ah,' exclaimed Cyrus Smith: 'If you can cry, it means that you have once more become a man!' "

"How fine that is!" said Monsieur Bordas. "It all comes back to me now. Isn't the island attacked by convicts?"

"Yes, and it's Ayrton who first catches sight of the black flag. . . . Would you like me to go on reading?"

The schoolmaster pushed his chair still further back. He could, he should, have been lost in wonder at sound of the ardent voice coming from this boy who was generally regarded as an idiot. He could, he should, have rejoiced in the task that had been laid upon him, at the power that was his to save this trembling scrap of humanity. But he heard the boy only through the tumult of his own thoughts. . . . Here he was, a man of forty, burning with desires, bursting with ideas, yet fated never to escape from a schoolhouse in an empty village street. He could understand and appraise all that was printed in the magazine. The smell of its ink and gum was in his nostrils. All the questions of which it treated were familiar to him, though he could talk of them to nobody but Monsieur Lousteau. There was a lot, too, that Léone could have grasped, but she preferred her daily chores. Her mind was growing indolent as her physical activities increased. It had become a matter of pride to her that she could scarcely keep her eyes open when evening came, so tired did she feel. Sometimes she was filled with pity for her husband, for she was too intelligent not to realize that he was suffering. But in Jean-Pierre they would find their compensation. It was her opinion that when a man has reached her husband's age he is willing enough to shift the burden of ambition to the shoulders of his son . . . that was her opinion.

He noticed that the boy, having reached the end of the chapter, had stopped.

"Shall I go on?"

"No," said Monsieur Bordas, "take a rest. You read very well. Would you like me to lend you one of Jean-Pierre's books?"

Guillou jumped up and once again began to examine all the volumes, one by one, spelling out their titles in a low voice.

"*Sans famille* . . . is that a nice one?"

"Jean-Pierre used to be very fond of it. But he reads more serious books now."

The Weakling and the Enemy

"D'you think I should understand it?"

"Of course you would! My school work doesn't give me much time for reading nowadays. . . . You shall tell me what it's about, a bit each day. I shall enjoy that."

"That's what you say! . . . but I know you're laughing at me, really. . . ."

Guillou walked over to the fireplace. He looked at a photograph leaning against the mirror. It showed schoolboys grouped round two masters wearing pince-nez. Their trousers were stretched tight over their large knees. He asked whether Jean-Pierre was there.

"Yes, in the front row—to the right of the master."

He would have recognized him, thought Guillou, even if he had not been pointed out. Among all the other dim and meaningless faces, this one face glowed. Was it because of all he had been hearing about Jean-Pierre that he thought that? For the first time in his life, he was realizing what a human face could be like. He had often looked long and fondly at pictures, in love with the features of some figure of fiction. But now it suddenly came to him that this boy with the high forehead, the close curls, and the frown between his eyes, was the boy who had actually read these books, worked at this table, slept in this bed.

"Is this room really his very own? Can't anyone come into it if he doesn't want them to?"

He, himself, was never alone except in the lavatory. . . .

The rain was splashing on the roof. How lovely it must be to live all shut away among all these books . . . beyond. the reach of other people. But Jean-Pierre needed no defenses. He was top of his form in every subject. He had even won a prize for gymnastics, Monsieur Bordas had said.

Léone pushed the door open. "Your mother has come for you, young man."

Once more he followed on behind the schoolmaster carrying the lamp. Once more he crossed the family bedroom. Paula de Cernès was drying her shoes at the fire. She must have come by dirty field-paths. . . .

"No need for me to ask whether you got anything out of him. Of course you didn't!"

Monsieur Bordas protested that things hadn't gone badly at all. The boy stood with hanging head while Léone buttoned his cape.

"Would you mind coming outside with me for a moment?" said Paula. "It has left off raining, and I should like to know what you really think."

The schoolmaster took down his mackintosh. His wife followed him into their bedroom. He wasn't going to go stumping the roads at night with that madwoman, was he? He'd be getting himself talked about. . . . All this she asked, but only got a snub for her pains. Paula, who could guess the subject of their whispered conversation, pretended that she had heard nothing. At the front door she once again overwhelmed Léone with protestations of gratitude. Then, with the schoolmaster at her side, she plunged into the damp darkness. She said to Guillou:

"You run along ahead, and don't keep getting under our feet."

Her voice, when she turned to her companion, was firm and determined.

The Weakling and the Enemy

"I want to know the truth, no matter how painful the truth may be to a mother's ears."

He had slowed his pace. Might not Léone be right after all? Whatever happened, they mustn't be seen together crossing the path of light which came from the Hotel Dupuy. But even had he been certain that they would not be seen, he would still have been on the defensive. He had never been anything else with women, since the days of his boyhood. It had always been they who sought him out, always he who had run away —and not that he might be the more urgently pursued.

As they approached the Hotel Dupuy, he halted.

"We had better postpone this conversation till tomorrow. Come to my house toward the end of the morning. I finish at the *Mairie* just before noon."

She knew perfectly well why he did not want to walk further with her. The thought that there was something very like the beginning of a plot between them filled her with joy.

"Yes," she murmured; "that will be much better."

"Till tomorrow evening then, Guillaume, my boy. You shall read *Sans famille* to me."

Monsieur Bordas did no more than raise one finger to his beret. Almost at once he was lost to sight, but Paula could still hear, from time to time, the noise made by his stick striking a stone. The boy too remained for a few moments motionless in the middle of the road, gazing back at the light which came from Jean-Pierre's home.

His mother took him by the arm. She asked him no questions. There was nothing to be got out of him. Besides, what did she care? Tomorrow they were to have their first meeting, their first intimate talk. She gripped Guillou's little hand more tightly than she need have done. The cold of the rain-drenched road struck through her shoes.

"Come to the fire," said Fraülein; "you're soaked to the skin."

Every eye was fixed on him. He would have to answer all their questions.

"Well, so your schoolmaster didn't gobble you up after all?"

He shook his head.

"What did you do for those two hours?"

He did not know what to say. What *had* he done? His mother pinched his arm.

"Didn't you hear? What did you do for those two hours?"

"I shelled beans."

The Baronne raised her hands.

"So he shelled beans for them! A nice thing, I must say!" she said, unconsciously imitating her Arbis grandchildren. "Do you hear that, Paula? The schoolmaster and his wife sit there gloating, while *my* grandson shells their beans for them! Just what·I might have expected. Perhaps they asked you to sweep out the kitchen?"

"No, Mamie. I only shelled beans. A lot had gone bad, and I had to sort them out."

"It didn't take them long to size him up!" said Paula. ·

Fraülein protested: "I think it was only that they didn't want to scare him the first day."

But the Baronne knew what was to be expected from people like that once they had got anyone in their clutches.

"No doubt it gives them a great deal of pleasure to play a trick like that on us. But if they think they've got the better

63

of me, they're very much mistaken. I don't mind in the least."

"If they treated Guillou badly . . ." broke in Fraülein sharply, "I am very sure that Madame la Baronne would not tolerate it . . . after all, he is her own grandson. . . ."

Guillou's voice rose shrill: "The schoolmaster isn't a bad man!"

"Because he made you shell beans? . . . you like doing servant's work . . . you like being a good-for-nothing. . . . But he's going to make you read, and write and do sums . . . and with him," went on Paula, "you'll have to watch how you go. Don't forget that he's a schoolmaster!"

In a low, trembling voice Guillou stuck to his point. "He isn't a bad man . . . he's made me read already . . . and he says I read well."

But his mother, Mamie and Fraülein had begun bickering again, and were not listening.

All right, then, what did he care? He'd *keep* his secret. The schoolmaster had made him read *The Mysterious Island*. Tomorrow he was going to start on *Sans famille*. Every evening now he would go to Monsieur Bordas' house. He could look at Jean-Pierre's photograph for as long as he liked. Already he adored Jean-Pierre madly. They would become friends during the summer holidays. He would turn the pages of all Jean-Pierre's books, one by one, the books which Jean-Pierre's hands had touched. It was not because of Monsieur Bordas that his heart was overflowing with happiness, but because of an unknown boy. The sense of delight never left him for the whole evening. It was with him during the interminable meal, at which the irascible gods sat, separated by deserts of silence, during which Guillou could hear Galéas chewing and swallowing. It stayed with him while he groped his way out of his clothes between the dressmaker's dummy and the sewing machine, while he lay shivering between his stained sheets, when he began his prayers all over again because he had not paid attention to the meaning of the words, and when he had to struggle against the temptation of lying on his stomach. . . . Long after sleep had come, a smile still lit the child's face, that was like the face of an old man, with moist and pendulous lips. It was a smile which might have filled his mother with surprise had she been one of those women who tuck their children up in bed, and leave a blessing with them for the night.

About the same time, Léone broke in on her husband's reading.

"Look!" she exclaimed, "what that filthy little creature has done to Jean-Pierre's book! There are finger marks all over it, and even traces of nose-dirt! What can have come over us to lend him Jean-Pierre's books!"

"There's nothing particularly sacrosanct about them . . . You're not the mother of the Messiah!"

Léone, now thoroughly put out, raised her voice:

"I won't have the little horror here again! You can give him his lessons in the schoolroom, in the stables, anywhere you like, but not here!"

Robert shut his book, got up, went across, and sat down beside his wife in front of the fire.

"You're not exactly a model of consistency, are you? Only a little while ago you were blaming me because I showed the old Baronne the door, and now you've got a grievance because

The Weakling and the Enemy

I behaved decently to her daughter-in-law. . . . It's the bearded lady that's the trouble . . . it's no use your denying it . . . poor bearded lady!"

"And don't *you* deny that it'd be a fine feather in your cap!" said Léone, giving him a kiss. "I know you. What a scalp to hang at your belt—the lady from the great house!"

"I really don't think I could bring it off, not even if I wanted to."

"Oh I know all about what differentiates men," said Léone; "you've explained it to me often enough. There are those who are always ready for it, and those who aren't . . ."

"Yes, and those who are always ready, don't, really, live for anything else, because, whatever people may say, it's about the pleasantest thing in life."

"And those who aren't," said Léone, continuing with the litany (there were several "gags," dating from the days when they were first engaged, which they were always trotting out, because they could always be relied upon to bring every argument to a happy end), "devote themselves to God, to Science, or to Literature. . . ."

"Or to their own sex," wound up Robert. She laughed and went into the bathroom, leaving the door open. As he was undressing, he called out to her:

"You know, I wouldn't have minded taking on the little wretch . . . might have been interesting."

She came back looking pleased with herself and rather appealing in her faded red flannel nightgown, with her rather lifeless hair braided in a plait.

"Then you've given up the idea?"

"If I have, it's not because of the bearded lady! But I've

been thinking . . . I'll have to go back on my promise. I ought never to have given it in the first place. We mustn't have anything to do with the great house. The class-war isn't just something in a textbook. It's part of our daily life, and it ought to control our every action."

He broke off. She was squatting on her heels, cutting her toenails. She was quite determined not to listen.

". . . One can't talk to women . . ."

The mattress creaked under the weight of his large body. She snuggled up against him and blew out the candle. The room was filled with the smell of burned wick. It was a smell they both of them loved, because it was the precursor of lovemaking and sleep.

"No, not tonight," said Léone.

They whispered for a while.

"Stop talking now, I'm going to sleep."

"Just one more thing: how on earth am I going to get that urchin off my hands?"

"All you've got to do is write a note to the bearded lady, explaining all about the class-war. She'll understand all right . . . after all, she *was* a Mademoiselle Meulière! . . . We'll send one of the kids round with it tomorrow. . . . Look, it's hardly dark at all!"

Cocks were crowing to one another. In the linen closet of the great house, where Fraülein had forgotten to draw the curtains, the moon shone down on Guillou, a pale little ghost perched on his chamber-pot. Behind him, armless, headless, stood the dummy which no one ever used.

4

THE note delivered by one of the schoolchildren had brought his mother and Mamie much earlier than usual from their rooms. They had the terrible appearance of old people early in the morning, before they had washed, and while their discolored teeth, embedded in pink, are still reposing in tumblers of water by their bedsides. Mamie's scalp looked smooth and polished between her thin strands of faded hair, and her empty mouth made it seem as though she were sucking in her cheeks. They were both talking at the same time. Galéas, seated at table, between his two hounds—whose jaws snapped every time he threw them a scrap of food—was drinking his coffee as though it hurt him. To see him, one would think that every mouthful was an agony. It was Guillaume's firm conviction that the enormous Adam's apple prevented the food from going down. He kept his mind concentrated on his father. He did not want to understand the meaning of the heated words now passing between his mother and Mamie on the subject of the note. But he knew already that he would never again enter Jean-Pierre's room.

"That wretched little Communist teacher's nothing to do with me!" exclaimed Mamie. "It's *you* he's written to. This snub is aimed at you, my dear."

"What do you mean—snub? He is reading me a lesson. It

is a lesson I needed, and I'm glad of it. I believe in the class-war just as much as he does. I didn't mean him any harm. Still, I did urge him to betray his own people."

"What on earth you're getting at, my poor dear, I do *not* know!"

"Here's a young man with all his life before him, and every reason to hope for a brilliant future. And what do I do? I try to compromise him in the eyes of his comrades and his Party leaders . . . And for what, I ask you? . . . For the sake of a little backward degenerate. . . ."

"I am present, Paula."

She guessed at, rather than heard, her husband's protest. He was still sitting crouched over his bowl of bread and milk. When he grew excited, his thick tongue gave passage only to a confused muddle of sound. Raising his voice, he added: "Guillaume happens to be present too."

"The things one's got to listen to!" exclaimed Fraülein, and vanished into the scullery.

By this time, the old Baronne had recovered her breath.

"So far as I know, Guillaume is your son too!"

Hatred had quickened the senile jerking of the aged head which was bare and bald and prepared already for the noth-ingness of death.

Paula whispered in her ear: "Just look at them both—the original and the copy. It's extraordinary how alike they are!"

The Baronne straightened her back, looked her daughter-in-law up and down without replying, and then, with not a word to Guillou, got up and left the kitchen. The child's gray little face expressed nothing at all. There was a fog outside, and, since Fraülein never washed the one and only window, almost the only light in the room came from the flickering logs in the grate. . . . The two hounds with their muzzles on their paws, and the rough-hewn legs of the enormous table, looked for a moment almost as though they were on fire.

Not another word was spoken. Paula had gone too far, as she fully realized, had affronted the great army of her husband's race, his thousand sleeping ancestors. Galéas uncurled his long legs, scrambled to his feet, wiped his mouth with the back of his hand, and asked the boy whether he had got his cape. He fastened it round the scrawny, birdlike neck, and took Guillou's hand in his. He kicked the two dogs awake. They leaped, fawning on him, all eagerness to follow. Fraülein asked where they were off to. Paula took the words out of his mouth:

"Oh, to the churchyard, of course!"

Yes, that was where they were going. A red sun was struggling with the fog which might lift later, or dissolve in rain. Guillou clung to his father's hand, but very soon had to let it go because it was so damp. Not a word did they exchange until they reached the Church. The family tomb of the Cernès stood against the churchyard wall from which the eye could look across the Ciron valley. Galéas went off to fetch a spade from the sacristy. The boy sat down on a gravestone at some little distance from the tomb. He pulled the hood of his cape over his head, then moved no more. . . . Monsieur Bordas didn't want to have anything more to do with him. The fog was acting like a sounding-board. He could hear a distant wagon, a crowing cock, the monotonous drone of a motor car, above the unbroken threshing of the mill-wheel, and the roar of the weir, near which, in summer time, the village boys bathed naked. A robin sang quite close to him. The migrant birds he loved had flown. Monsieur Bordas didn't want to have anything more to do with him. Not a soul, anywhere, wanted him. "I don't care," he said in a low voice, and then, again, as though in challenge to some unseen enemy—"I don't care!" What a noise the weir was making—it was less than a kilometer away as the crow flies. A sparrow winged its way out of the Church through the broken window. "The Good God isn't there"—that was what Mamie said: "They have taken the Good God away. . . ." He was nowhere else, only up in the sky. Dead children are like angels, with pure and shining faces. Guillou's tears, said Mamie, were dirty tears. The more he cried, the filthier his face became, because his grubby hands smeared it with earth. When he got home, his mother would say . . . Mamie would say . . . Fraülein would say . . .

Monsieur Bordas wasn't going to have anything more to do with him. He would never again go into Jean-Pierre's room. Jean-Pierre. Jean-Pierre Bordas. How strange to love a boy whom one has never seen, and never will see. "If he had met me, he would have thought me ugly, dirty, stupid." That was what his mother told him every day: "You're ugly, dirty, stupid." Jean-Pierre Bordas would never know that Guillaume de Cernès was ugly, dirty, stupid—a ragamuffin. And he was something else, too. What was the word his mother had used just now?—a word which had struck his father like a stone? He tried to remember, and could think only of "regenerate." It was some word like "regenerate."

Tonight he would fall asleep, but not at once. He would have to wait for sleep, wait through a whole night like last night

71

when he had been trembling with happiness. He had fallen asleep thinking that when he woke he would see Monsieur Bordas again, that when evening came, he would sit in Jean-Pierre's room and start to read *Sans famille*. . . . If only he could believe that tonight everything would be as it had been then! . . . He got to his feet, made his way round the Cernès tomb, clambered over the wall, and took the path which went steeply downhill toward the Ciron.

Galéas turned his head and saw that the boy was no longer there. He went to the wall and looked over it. The little hood was moving among the vine rows, getting further and further away. He threw his spade aside and started off down the same path. When he was no more than a few yards from the boy, he slowed his pace. Guillou had thrown back his hood. He was not wearing a beret. Between his large, projecting ears his cropped head looked very small. His legs were like two twigs ending in enormous boots. His chicken neck stuck out above the cape. With his eyes Galéas devoured the little shambling creature, the tiny shrewmouse with marks of blood upon it of the trap from which it had escaped. It was his own son, his image in the flesh, with a whole life to live, yet now, already, burdened with a long-borne weight of suffering. But the torment had only just begun. The torturers would gain new strength. Those of childhood are different from those of youth; and there would be still others when he had become a man full grown. Could he learn to be numb and sottish? Would he have to defend himself, at every moment of his life, against the woman who would be always there, the woman with the Gorgon's face blotched with bilious yellow? Hatred caught at his breath, but, more than hatred, shame, because it was he who had been that woman's torturer. Only once had he taken her in his arms, only once. She was, now, like a bitch confined—not for a few days only. Through all her youth it had gone on, and for years and years she would go howling for the absent male. . . . With what fantasies . . . what actions . . . had he, Galéas, cheated hunger . . . Every night, yes, every night, and in the morning, too. . . . Such would be the lot of this abortion born of their one embrace, and now running, now hurrying—to what? Did he know? Though the child had not once turned his head, perhaps he was conscious of his father's presence. Galéas was persuaded that it was so! He knows I am behind him. He takes no pains to hide himself from me, no, nor to cover his tracks. He is as a guide, leading me to where he wants me to be with him! Galéas could not bring himself to face the issue to which these last two of the Cernès line were hastening. A tremble of alder leaves spoke of the nearby river. Not now was it the King of the Alders who, in a final gallop, was pursuing the boy, but the boy now who was leading his uncrowned and insulted father toward the sleeping waters of the weir, the pool in which the village boys, in summer, bathed naked. They were close now to the watery confines of that kingdom where never more would they be harassed by wife or mother. They would be delivered from the Gorgon; they would sleep.

They had reached the shade of the tall pines on the river bank. The still living bracken fronds were almost as high as Guillou, whose cropped head Galéas could scarcely see emerging from their tangled wilderness. At a turning of the sandy path the boy once more vanished from sight. They might have met some resin-gatherer, the muleteer from the mill, a

sportsman out after woodcock. But every witness had withdrawn from this small corner of the world that the act might
be accomplished which these two were fated to perform—one
leading the other? or urging him forward unwillingly?—
who would ever know? There was none to see them, but only
the giant pines crowding about the weir. They burned during
the following August, left too long untapped. For a long while
they spread their calcined limbs above the sleeping water; for
a long while they reared against the sky their blackened faces.

The accepted view was that Galéas had jumped into the
water to save his son, that the boy had clung about his neck
and pulled him down. Such vague rumors as had at first been
current were soon silenced by the touching story of a father
done to death by his small son's clutching hands. Some might
shake their heads and say . . . "Well, I don't feel sure that
it happened like that" . . . but the true explanation no one
could well imagine. How should anyone suspect a father who
loved his boy, and took him every day when he went to the
churchyard? . . . "Monsieur Galéas may have been a bit simple, but he had his wits about him all the same and there
never was a sweeter-natured man."

No one grudged Fraülein the cape which she had taken,
sodden with water, from Guillou's body. . . . The old Baronne
was happy to think that Cernès would descend to the Arbis
children, and that she would be quit, once and for all, of
Paula, to whom the Meulières had offered a home. She was,
as they put it, back on their hands. But she had a malignant
tumor. On the glossy walls, in the stifling atmosphere of the
hospital (the nurse forever coming in with the basin whether

74

she wanted it or not, and even if she was too tired to open her eyes—and the morphine which was so bad for her liver—and the visits of her aunt always worrying over the terrible expense, which was quite useless anyhow, because the end was a foregone conclusion)—on the glossy walls she sometimes saw, as on a screen, Galéas' shaggy head, and the brat looking up from a torn book, an ink-stained exercise, with his dirty, anxious face. Perhaps she imagined these things? She saw, in fancy, the boy creeping close to the bank, shivering because he was afraid, not of death, but of the cold—and his father tiptoeing behind him. . . . At that point she hesitated. Had he pushed him, or plunged after him?—or had he taken the small boy in his arms, saying, "Hold tight to me, and don't look." . . . Paula did not know, nor ever would. She was happy to think that her own death was close at hand. She kept on telling the nurse that the morphine made her feel ill, that her liver could not stand any more injections. She wanted to drain her cup to the dregs—not that she believed in an unseen world whither our victims precede us, where we can fall at the knees of those who were confided to our care, and have, through our fault, been lost. It never occurred to her that she might be judged. She stood at no bar save that of her own conscience. She was absolved in her own sight from the horror she had felt for a son who was the image of a hated father. She had spewed up the Cernès family, because nausea is something that one cannot control. But it was of her own free will that she had consented to share the bed of a half-impotent monster. She had allowed him to take her in his arms, and that, in her eyes, was the crime for which there was no pardon.

75

The Weakling and the Enemy

Sometimes the pain was so acute that she could not resist the morphine's promise of a moment's respite. In those lucid intervals she thought of all the lives she might have had. In fancy she was Robert Bordas' wife, surrounded by a brood of healthy boys, whose lower lips did not hang down, who did not slaver. Each night he took her in his arms, and she slept pressed close to his body. She dreamed of men's hairy pelts, and of their smell. She never knew what time of day or night it was. Pain knocked at the door; pain entered in and took its lodgement, and started slowly to eat her life away.

That a mother should be ashamed of her son, or of her grandson, should not, thought Fraülein, be permitted. She could not forgive her mistress for having shed so few tears over Galéas and Guillou having gone, for having, perhaps, been happy at their going. But Madame la Baronne would pay a heavy price. The Arbis family would never let her die in peace at Cernès. "Suppose I told Madame la Baronne what I heard their chauffeur say after the funeral—about how could anyone think that a woman of her age could possibly need a gardener, an assistant gardener, and two indoor servants, and all the expenses of a house? That is how their minds are working. I know that they have been inquiring about terms for aged pensioners of the Ladies of the Presentation at Verdelais." . . . The Baronne kept turning and twisting her bald vulture's head among the pillows. She would refuse to go to the Ladies of the Presentation . . . If the Arbis have decided, Madame la Baronne will go, and I with her. Madame la Baronne has never been able to say "no" to the Arbis. They frighten her; and, I confess, they frighten me.

The Weakling and the Enemy

Thursday: a respite from the children. But the schoolmaster had his work to do at the *Mairie*. Hurriedly he passed a washing glove over his face which was puffy with sleep. What point was there in shaving? Nobody who mattered would see him. He did not put on walking shoes. In weather like this a pair of socks would keep his feet warm, and with clogs on, he need not fear getting them wet. Léone had gone to the butcher's. He could hear the rain upon the roof. There was a puddle right across the road. When Léone got back, she would say, "What are you thinking about?" and he would answer "nothing." They had not so much as mentioned Guillou's name since the day when the two bodies had been fished out of the mill-pond. Then, for the first and only time, he had said: "The lad killed himself, or else his father . . ." and Léone with a shrug had muttered, "Do you really think so?" From then on, they had never mentioned the boy's name. But Léone knew that the little skeleton in cape and hood was forever wandering through the school, and creeping about the playground, not joining in the games. Robert Bordas went into Jean-Pierre's room, and took up *The Mysterious Island*. The book opened of itself. ". . . the poor wretch was about to plunge into the creek which lay between him and the forest. For a brief moment, his legs were like two springs at the moment of release . . . But almost at once he fell back, half collapsing, and a large tear welled up in his eye. 'Ah,' exclaimed Cyrus Smith: 'if you can cry, it means that you have once more become a man!' " . . . Monsieur Bordas sat down on Jean-Pierre's bed. The thick red book with its golden titling lay open on his knee. . . . Guillou . . . In that suffering body a human spirit

77

had lain unawakened. How wonderful to have helped it into consciousness. That, maybe, was the task which Robert Bordas had been born into this world to accomplish. At the Ecole Normale, one of the professors had taught Etymology—*Instituteur*—schoolmaster—from *Institutor*—one who builds, one who instructs, one who sets the human spirit in a man. A fine word. He might meet other Guillous on his road. For the sake of the child whom he had left to die, he would never again refuse to give of his utmost to those who came to him. But none of them would be that same small boy who now was dead because Monsieur Bordas had one day taken him in, and the next, had thrown him out like a stray puppy that he had warmed a moment at his fire. He had sent him into the darkness forever. But was it really darkness? He strained his eyes in an effort to see beyond material things, beyond the walls and the furniture of this, his house, beyond the tiled roof, beyond the star-pointed night, beyond the winter constellations. He sat there, seeking the kingdom of the spirit where, rapt away into eternity, the boy could see him still, and on his cheek, stubbly with unshaven beard, a tear he had not thought to wipe away.

The spring grass strayed into the churchyard at Cernès. Roots took hold upon the untended graves; moss made the epitaphs unreadable. Since the day when Galéas had taken his small son by the hand, choosing that they should sleep together, there had been nobody at Cernès to concern himself about the dead.

THE ENEMY

1

IT WAS the habit of Madame Dézaymeries to get up at day-
break and, after Mass, to waken Fabien with a kiss. The kiss
tasted of church and smelt of fog. The child loved the light,
as of some unknown land, that showed in his mother's eyes.
Each afternoon, when he got back from the park, she took him
to the Cathedral for the Holy Hour. He watched her lips,
convinced that she must be seeing God because she never
stopped talking to Him. Fabien was conscious of the boredom
of the passing moments, but there was in them, too, a quality
of pleasure. He pretended that his right hand was a woman
whom he was loading with necklaces. These necklaces were a
rosary. A priest passed under a canopy, preceded by a small
boy. A bell tinkled. The figures of the faithful turned, with a
noise of scraping chairs, toward this manifestation of the Presence. When the Monstrance gleamed in the middle of its six
candles, Madame Dézaymeries did not kneel, but stood, head
up, looking God straight in the face.

When evening came, she walked up and down the passage,
her rosary twined about her fingers. She held it stretched between her two hands, like a skein of wool, the better to see
the point she had reached in her "telling." Fabien followed
behind, holding up her dress, which he liked to imagine was
of silk brocade. Night began for him with the evening prayer.

The Weakling and the Enemy

His mother put him to bed, made the sign of the Cross on his forehead with her thumb, crossed his hands on his breast, and listened while he repeated the ritual sentences that should guard him against the threat of sudden death. She did not scruple to let him see the possibility that sleep might open straight into the endless vistas of eternity. His life followed the rhythm of the liturgical year. When the candles were lit round the Manger, he became a shepherd. On Holy Thursday he kneeled before the stripped altar, hearing with mingled terror and delight the lamentations of Jeremiah, and watching the candles of yellow wax go out one by one. The bells on Resurrection Morning danced with the gaiety of life reborn. The air of the Month of Mary filled his nostrils with the scent of white roses. No somber weight lay upon his life. Austerity wreathed it like a mist shot through with sunlight. No fears of hell-fire troubled him, nor yet of purgatory, since no Indulgence was neglected, and he drew with method on the treasures of the Faith.

Joseph, his fifteen-year-old elder brother, took delight in games that foreshadowed his vocation, games in which altars, processions and sermons played the principal parts. He was at boarding school, and came home only on Sundays after Vespers. The prevalent view was that, thin and overgrown though he was, he had a constitution of iron because he had escaped whooping cough, mumps, measles and all the childish ailments to which Fabien owed many periods of dreamy happiness during which he lived the life of a lazy and pampered Prince. But sickness of quite another kind was laying in wait for Joseph. It was, indeed, already at work in his system, though, for the time being, the only sign of its presence was what

The Weakling and the Enemy

Madame Dézaymeries called a "shocking cold" which the local nursing Sister treated with a daily spoonful of "Tolu" syrup. Fabien sought his company but rarely, and as a rule only when, after making his confession and tortured by scruples lest he might not have described certain of his faults in sufficient detail, he went to him for comfort. Quite often he would deliberately munch a blade of grass before Mass, or swallow a mouthful of water when he cleaned his teeth, so as to avoid having to take Communion, so fearful was he of committing sacrilege. Joseph was always very indignant at such tricks.

Madame Dézaymeries' Spiritual Director had a little talk with Fabien every day. He did not wear his stole on these occasions, and was careful to smile throughout the interview. With nothing of aggressiveness in his manner, but with an air of determination which was never oppressive, he had so worked on Madame Dézaymeries that she had grown to regard her widowhood as a species of religious vocation. He had set before this family of three the goal of perfection, and kept them isolated in a hedged and cloistered life. They visited none but the poor, and limited their social existence to official contacts with the clergy of the parish, about whom, Madame Dézaymeries sometimes went so far as to maintain, there was nothing supernatural. As President of the Christian Mothers, and Vice-President of the Ladies of Charity, she lent her drawing room for meetings so little worldly that the dust-sheets were never taken off the chairs, and the chandelier in its protective envelope hung like Montgolfier's balloon, motionless beneath a ceiling that prevented it from rising.

This pious routine had such a hold on Fabien that even at school, whither he went when he was about thirteen, he was

83

completely untroubled by the prickings of the flesh. Hints and murmured revelations fell dead on the threshold of his heart, and penetrated no further. He was entirely without interest in the things of the body, and was blessed with a divine stupidity in all matters that had to do with the vice of sensual indulgence. A saintly woman kept her hand in front of his eyes and shut him away from any vision of the world. He was wholly without knowledge of the powers that lurk within us, of the strident clamor of desire, of the storm that rages about the ship of humanity when God slumbers in the stern. But no woman can, unaided, make a man. Madame Dézaymeries, happy in her contemplation of the innocent and tranquil face that Fabien bent about his books, was blind to the fact that his arms were not so weak as Joseph's, nor his chest so hollow. At fifteen his boy's head with its brown hair sat ill upon his sturdy frame. She forgot that another than herself had had a share in the forming of this young creature whose expression was so pure, though he was over-given to dreaming; who was so scornful of bodily activities though built for physical prowess; who was content to live in ignorance of a body which stood already on the threshold of manhood.

She never spoke to her sons of their father, who had died shortly before Fabien was born. Yet the boy had only to look at his strong peasant bones, at his large, well-formed hands and wrists, at the muscles that were so tough for all their lack of exercise, to get some inkling of the nature of the unknown man who had given him life. Though the two boys had been brought up entirely by their mother, their movements were those of "poor papa," and the thick tones and country intonations of their voices belonged to him. Like him they were slow of step and seemingly docile to all external authority. But, deep down, they were reserved and inaccessible. Up to the age of twenty they knew nothing of the denizens of this world—with one exception. As the result of some curious aberration, their mother had given the freedom of the family circle to a stranger. Twice in each year, between Christmas and the New Year, and again in the middle of July, she shot across their night-sky, like one of those stars whose trajectory can be plotted in advance, leaving a trail of brilliance.

She had only to ring the front-door bell for the boys to go scampering from the fireside. "It's Fanny Barrett! It's Fanny!" they would cry in the hall. A distillation of perfume hung about her furs. For a moment she pressed her veiled face to Madame Dézaymeries' shoulder. A pastry cook and a waiter always came with her, because she feared that the dinner prepared for her might be insufficient. Fabien long remembered the labels on her bags, "Wanted on Voyage." It seemed to him as though the salt of all the oceans of the world had eaten into them. Toys, sweets and books made their appearance to a wonderful and rustling accompaniment of tissue paper. Octavie got the green room ready—that spare room that was spared only for Fanny.

The children knew that Fanny Barrett had been left an orphan, had moved from Dublin, her native city, and had come to the great port on the southwest coast of France where her uncle, on whom the duty of bringing her up had devolved, was associated in business with their Dupouy grandfather. At that time, Madame Dézaymeries, or, as she then was, Thérèse Dupouy, had the reputation of being a gawky girl of devout tendencies. Her father and mother, though rich, lived in self-imposed poverty. The only pleasure they would countenance, whether for themselves or for others, was that of "putting money aside." This they regarded as being the highest of all virtues. Old Dupouy had trained his wife in the ethics of economy so successfully that their house, filled with old trunks, disused bottles and empty packing-cases, had at first the dusty, overcrowded appearance of one of those dwellings where nothing is ever lost or thrown away. An elder and detestable sister had succeeded in casting a blight on Thérèse's youth. The Dupouys were one of those "good families" the members of which can endure one another only by behaving as miracles of virtue, who put up with this present life simply and solely because they believe in a better life to come. On each first Thursday in the month, Monsieur Maggie, Dupouy's partner, who was held in horror by the family because of his dissolute life (he kept a *première danseuse* called Mademoiselle Lovati, who cost him a hundred louis a month), was always at his wits' end to know what to do with his niece Fanny during her twelve hours' exeat from the Convent. He handed her over, therefore, to the tender mercies of the gloomy Thérèse, much as he might have given her a tame bird, and very soon a passionate devotion grew up between the two girls. The Dupouy parents dared not object to a charge of such manifest piety, but they grew to dread those recurring Thursdays which filled their melancholy abode with gusts of laughter and the sound of young feet racing up and down the passages. Much later, when Fanny, now of age and her own mistress, returned from Ireland after a long period of eclipse, to visit her great friend who was already a widow and the mother of two sons, living in what had once been the Dupouy, but was now the Dézaymeries' house, Thérèse blamed herself for having been too indulgent toward the faults of her junior, whose coquetry, petulance and excessive fondness for caresses she had, in the past, gone so far as to encourage. Particularly was she conscious of a sense of guilt in that she had taken so little heed of her companion's neglect of everything that touched upon religion. But this early love had left deep traces in her character, as was proved by the fact that she still remained loyal to it and shut her eyes to what, in anybody else, she would have regarded as an abomination.

The Irish girl had married an officer of the Royal Navy, but spoke of him as little as possible. She wandered about the world as freely as though she had been a widow. The Dézaymeries' knew nothing of her vagabond existence, and were completely unaware that she had been, for some time, separated from her husband, that she busied herself with selling curios in every capital of Europe, and that for many years she had lived comfortably off the proceeds of a trip to the Far East from which she had returned with a quantity of lacquer.

Her independence worried Madame Dézaymeries far less than did her lack of religion. It was not so much that she was actively hostile as utterly indifferent. For her the problem of religion just had no existence. On one occasion she interrupted a lecture from Thérèse on the subject with a "But, darling, it's all so *improbable!*" Thérèse found it convenient to lay the blame on Fanny's husband—an Anglican by birth but an atheist by temperament—and persuaded herself that it was her duty not to scare her friend away, but, by giving her a warm welcome, to lead her all unsuspecting to the Manger. The truth of the matter was that the widow clung to the younger woman because she represented the only tenderness of feeling she had ever known. When, after their mother's death, the family estate had been broken up, there had been a breach between Thérèse and her sister, since when no one had ever dreamed of giving her a kiss except her children and this same Fanny whose lack of all religious feeling she chose to regard as a natural infirmity. Fabien, already clearer-sighted than his mother, found this characteristic of her childhood friend at once attractive and terrifying. He hung about the alluring visitor whose error was, to all seeming, invincible. No argument had the slightest effect on her. It was as though she had no part nor lot in the sin of Adam, as though her tiny, isolated destiny were moving to its predestined end in a world that knew nothing of redemption. God could appeal neither to her heart nor to her reason; not but what she was a philosopher and prided herself on a liking for abstract ideas.

She had, all the same, when she was staying with the Dézaymeries, to acquiesce in Friday fasts and Sunday observances. "But why," she would say, half joking, half in earnest, "but why make life gloomier than it is already?" To such remarks Thérèse would reply by pointing out how useless it was to shut one's eyes to the fact that the world is a place full of suffering, to which Christ alone can give meaning and value. The Irish girl merely laughed and gave her dear friend a kiss.

She was fonder of Fabien than of Joseph and marked her preference by constant fondlings. Only a superstitious, a morbid, craving for contrast could explain the attraction which, twice every year, brought this lover of beauty into a cribbed and Jansenist provincial home. She would descend upon it with a flapping of weary wings. No doubt an emotional loyalty which nothing could altogether destroy had something to do with her behavior. She might be the slave of her desires, but it so happened that some of her desires were good. Her first and perhaps her only really pure passion had found its object in a young girl. Each year she wandered back to this clear source of refreshment, known only to herself, and bathed her hot hands and painted face in its icy waters.

But a year came when, unknown to herself, a change of emphasis took place in that love which had the power to bring her back from the far places of Europe. Was it for Thérèse Dézaymeries that she came, or for the boy who once, on a July afternoon, in the shuttered drawing room which the two lads believed to be sacred to the spirit of their dead father, had roughly broken from the two bare arms so fondly twined about his neck? Though not fully aware of the peril, Madame Dézaymeries was conscious of a vague feeling of alarm. She felt its presence deep within her, could *smell* the spiritual threat. Fabien, in a mood of childish fun not wholly innocent, would creep away and smoke the butt-ends of Fanny's drugged and scented cigarettes. His mother, always scrupulous in her judgments, was careful to avoid any suspicion that might incriminate her friend. To her she was still the unsophisticated little companion who had clung to her in the old days, nor would she let anything disturb that happy memory. But it was not altogether easy to maintain such an attitude, and again and again she would say to herself, though with dwindling conviction, "There's no evil in her . . . it's just that we're not used to her ways." Another of her self-deceiving phrases was: "She's such an oddity." Experience had never taught her that vice may often hide behind eccentricity, and lurk in the shadow of quiddities and affectations. Loyalty to this affection, in which God had no share, was her secret weakness. Trained though she was to examine her conscience with meticulous care, accustomed though she might be to explore with morbid and meticulous intensity the motives of her every thought, she always averted her eyes from the special corner of her heart where her tender affection for Fanny dwelt. Had their visitor ever been guilty of carelessness, the Dézaymeries might have been warned to be on their guard. But it amused her to adapt herself to the exigencies of their cloistered life. She chose her dresses and disciplined her tongue with the sole object of charming her Christian hosts.

She did not know that her spirit gave off a smell. When she went away she left behind her a troubled odor which hung about the very air that Madame Dézaymeries breathed. As, when the shot bird has vanished, a scrap of fluff among the dead leaves will show the sportsman where it is lying, so Fabien's melancholy languors were full of meaning to her. She noted his silences. Where the lovely bird had fallen, the boy's heart bore, as it were, a physical mark. On the pretext of wanting to be undisturbed, he insisted on doing his lessons in the green room, which was never heated and had a northerly aspect. He rummaged in the dressing-table drawers and hoarded as treasure-trove forgotten ribbons and a tortoiseshell comb.

At last, when Fabien was sixteen, Madame Dézaymeries had her eyes opened. That year Fanny Barrett did not pay her accustomed visit. Each evening between Christmas and the New Year Fabien was on the watch, his face pressed to the window, or lurking on the landing, his ears pricked for the sound of a footstep. Joseph, who had always instinctively avoided Fanny, poked gentle fun at him. Of the three of them, he, already a priest at heart, already a sworn enemy of those lost women who have it in their power to bring damnation into unfledged lives, was by far the most sensitively alive to the corruption which she carried about with her. One evening, when the two brothers were deep in an argument, Joseph maintaining that to paint one's face was a deadly sin, their mother had had to silence them. After the New Year, Fabien begged her to write to Fanny at the various addresses she had left. The boy's general taciturnity, the prolonged silences into which he fell, were a sign that all was not as it should be, and she became alarmed. Finally, she confided in her Spiritual Director. The good Father continued to smile as usual, because his smile was a permanent feature of his face which nothing would ever erase, but his words expressed a deep displeasure. She had, he said, locked in the wolf with the sheep. Her care for the young soul in her charge had been of no avail, because the Evil One had been able to sow his seed at leisure. So shaken did she seem to be by his reproof that he felt bound to soften the hard words he had spoken, and to this end added that, since it was Fabien's destiny to live in the world, it might be no bad thing that he should learn the nature of its illusory charms. The mother's imprudence might, God willing, serve, after all, to insure the boy's salvation. All the same, he warned her to turn this temporary separation to good account, and to see to it that the friendship should be permanently discontinued.

The priest had little difficulty in bringing Fabien to a calmer state of mind. But the only effect of this was that the boy showed less confidence than ever in his mother, avoiding her questions, and, though he appeared to have lowered his defenses, was in fact more wary than ever. During the Easter holidays, which were spent as usual on the Dézaymeries' country estate some twenty miles from the city, he developed a strong liking for solitary walks. He would set off alone through the pine woods and spend long days out on the heath which, though it formed part of his father's property, was, with its sandy distances, its straight, tall tree trunks gashed with resin-oozing scars, a visible symbol of his mother's teaching. Nothing more arid than this countryside could well be imagined, nothing more featureless, more uniform. Yet, for all that, it is a land of hidden springs with waters stained red by the stony soil. Ice-cold, they bubble up beneath the overshadowing alders and in the thickets of wild mint. Just so is the human heart, trained by the will to woo austerity, but thrilling to the call of love and informed by grace. When evening fell the silence was so complete that the ear could catch the movement of the hidden streams on the surface of which lay long trails of slowly moving weed that looked like the hair of drowned and vanquished nymphs held prisoner by depths of stainless sand and washed by freshets. Giant pines made a circle of gloom about the house. As straitly as by the high walls of the Catholic faith, by its unbreached and solid doctrine, the Dézaymeries' lived hemmed about by the endless army of the pines which stood in serried ranks for forty miles. Only in that far distance did an ultimate ridge of sand lie as a barrier against the ocean surge. No austere heart is less responsive to the lure of passion than is this countryside to the magic of spring. The stunted oaks greet the winds of April with a rustle of dead leaves, and only the song of birds is eloquent of love.

Madame Dézaymeries felt a deep concern at these lonely expeditions from which Fabien would return with bleeding hands, and sometimes with dead leaves in his hair. She was alarmed to find that she felt lost when he was not with her, and that the companionship of Joseph brought her no comfort. Joseph, at this time, was a thin, tall youth who walked with a stoop, knew the names of all the curés of all the parishes of the diocese, and found his chief pleasure in playing on a miniature harmonium.

It was in the course of these holidays that, realizing her preference for Fabien, she sternly sat in judgment on her feelings and decided that her much-loved son must be sent away from home. She saw only too well what joy it would be for her to grow old with him beside her, and indulged herself with the thought that she might suffer the more by rejecting the sweet temptation. She began to speak to him of the École des Chartes, which was the obvious goal of anyone who had so strong a taste for the history of the Middle Ages. In this way her passion for self-sacrifice led her to plan the establishment of her son in that city where every passion can be gratified.

No incident came to disturb the family circle, where Fanny Barrett's name was no longer mentioned. In July Fabien took his baccalaureate, and the family removed once again to the country. There, in Les Landes, the sand concentrates the heat of heaven, and the crowding trees present a barrier that stops and turns aside the promise of cool breezes. All three were so consumed by inner heat as to be insensible to the torrid weather. Joseph, when daylight ebbed, rehearsed the reading of his breviary with the aid of a black-bound book crammed with sacred pictures. Fabien avoided his brother, but could not escape the rigor of the dog-days. In the pitiless blaze of noon he would lie with a book by Père Gratry on the bank of the stream where the warm moisture of the spongy moss brought refreshment to his body. The heathy wastes were filled with the tumult of ci-

The Weakling and the Enemy

cadas. Blue or tawny dragonflies hovered above the bracken fronds. Now and again the play of squirrels would set the motionless tree-tops momentarily swaying. Imprisoned among the gashed, tormented trunks, where his dreaming mind could find no outlet from the constricting sand, Fabien knew that nothing would come to shatter the drowsy peace of the afternoon save possibly the breathless sound of tocsin bells warning of heath fires. The merciless season of late summer makes the promise of autumn seem like a breath of deliverance. The first shower brings respite alike to earth and human flesh. The rain patters on the branches with a sound of happy tears. The drops, caught in their fall and absorbed by all the sickly leaves, never reach the sandy, burned-up surface of the earth. Westward, the pine trunks stand in black array, whipped by brief squalls borne on the bitter wind.

But in Fabien's heart it was August still, and he burned with a passion that he did not understand.

In October Joseph was received into the Seminary at Issy-les-Moulineaux. A little later it was Fabien's turn to depart. One November evening, his mother, stern in her resolve not to see him off on the Paris train, touched his forehead with the kiss which was her habitual talisman for the perilous passage of the hours of darkness. So successfully did she disguise her emotion that he dared not exhibit his own. But when at last, among the noises of the city, she could no longer hear the sound of the fly that was taking him from her, she let her widowed glance play about the vacant room. The lamp shone only on an empty chair. Octavie had already made her bed ready for the night. The hideous curtains of deep purple that masked the windows looked black.

2

EVEN when Fabien, in the early hours, stood shivering on the platform of the d'Orsay station, his suitcase in his hand, the climate of his mind remained unaltered. He was imprisoned at the center of a cocoon spun by his mother and by his Spiritual Director. How, then, was it possible that he should feel the impact of Paris? In the hotel where he was lodged, close to the Catholic Institute, he was forever passing bishops on the stairs, tottering old men leaning on the arms of discreetly dressed valets. There was a prevailing smell of vegetables which reminded him of school, nor in these musty odors of the kitchen was there any admixture of those scents that, in hotels of a different sort, fill the passages when the rooms are being "done." Such time as he did not spend at the École des Chartes, at the Record Office or the National Library he gave to a small group which existed for the study of social problems. But the theories and the formulæ which he read in various learned journals and glibly repeated, had no real hold on his secret self. They were merely an element of the mental atmosphere which kept him from the outside world. As a river may flow through a lake without becoming part of it, so did Fabien move through Paris. Of the ardors burning in the secret lives of men, ardors that may be glimpsed in the tense expressions of certain faces lit by the candle-light of Montmartre or of Notre-Dame-des-Victoires, he knew nothing. Never was a scrupulous Christian so empty of enthusiasm. He went so far as to take positive satisfaction in the sense of spiritual aridity which beset him, imagining that his feet were set upon that path of purification so well known to the mystics as desolate and comfortless. Strong in his Jansenist heritage, he held aloof from all contact with his fellow-students, never relaxing his hold upon his feelings, never seeking the intimacies of friendship, but meeting all advances with the cold detachment of his Dézaymeries training. He did not even make an effort to pay a visit to his brother at Issy. By sheer will-power he kept himself within the bleak rigidity of duty. But even so, he would often, of an evening, close his books and let his attention wander. The silence of the room spread till it held his very mind enveloped. He went to the window and drew the curtains aside. A frozen moon sailed above the city where millions of hearts were beating. The glass of the pane was cold to his forehead. He did not even try to pray, conscious that no words of love other than those contained in his prescribed evening devotions would rise to his lips. He was like a dry desert that is fully aware of its dryness. But, deep within himself he could catch, as from the distance of a torrid summer day, the echo of a muted rumbling. Fearful, yet with a stirring of hope, the listener says, "A storm is brewing"—a storm that will bruise the vine-shoots with its hail, but will bring, as well, relief to the dried and gaping earth, to the leaves drooping with the heat. Sometimes, so lonely was his state, he would fall so far as to listen to the confidences of the chambermaid who implored him to protect her from the unwelcome attentions of the "master," an uncouth and pasty sacristan, and of his sixteen-year-old son who had a flat head, looked like a louse, and was always lying in wait for her in the passage.

During Lent, Madame Dézaymeries paid a visit to Paris. He went with her to Issy, where Joseph, already suffering from his lungs and behindhand in his studies, sat coughing in the dark parlor under the painted stare of Sulpician worthies. He showed them the theatrical chapel—a sumptuous antechamber to the throne-room of the King of Kings. Fabien envied Joseph his life in this holy mountain, this tabernacle. It never occurred to him that, left to himself, he would have felt no wish to go and see him there. Madame Dézaymeries was filled with admiration of his virtue, of his active response to the charms of the perfect life even in the very heart of Paris. An experienced priest would have seen in it the ultimate rictus of a will absurdly stretched to breaking-point, and quite untouched by the spirit of love.

When he returned after the Easter holidays, Fabien began to take stock of his loneliness. The old stones of palaces and bridges lay basking in the soft radiance of a misty sun. The city was full of young bodies responsive to the call of spring, meeting at every corner, sitting on the terrace of every café. The air was full of stale romance. It was the time of year when the enemy within us finds a ready ally in the outward scene. To the moaning of desire repressed and stifled, nature replies with an invitation to escape, with a proffered gift of satisfaction. At the school even the most studious leaned gazing from the windows, their hands and their foreheads moist. A thousand strident posters called temptingly from sun-baked walls. It was that season when the streets are full of faces that no longer try to hide their secret yearnings, when parted lips and seeking eyes take no account of the dangerous abyss.

The Weakling and the Enemy

The threat of an approaching examination at first saved Fabien from himself. He tired his eyes with poring over fac-similes of ancient documents. In his brief snatches of leisure he dreamed of the moment, now close at hand, when his weariness would find rest in country air. Among all those motionless and wounded trees whose tops alone swayed gently, he would be but one wounded thing the more. Soon he would take his way to that land of scented heat. . . .

But, two days before he was due to start, a letter from his mother filled him with consternation. She told him to fetch Joseph from the Seminary, and to travel home with him. The boy had sent word that he was very ill, and his superiors had made no attempt to hide from Madame Dézaymeries the fact that there was very little hope indeed of saving the stripling priest. Fabien was overcome with terror when he saw the tall, emaciated body standing at the top of the main staircase at Issy, supported by two fellow-seminarists. If only he had kept a watchful eye on him, had not left him so utterly alone! The night that followed was horrible. Fabien lay in the upper bunk of their sleeper, hearing through the noises of the train his brother's paroxysms of coughing, and the sound of the spittoon rattling on the shelf.

For a day or two it seemed as though the air of the country would check the progress of the disease. But one night a sudden haemorrhage showed that it had returned with redoubled strength. The summer became a nightmare. The noise of coughing tore the siesta hours to shreds, and even the scent of the pines could not overpower the stench of iodoform, though the windows were always kept wide open. Madame Dézay-meries insisted on Fabien spending his days in the air, at the mercy of the hot sun. She stood at the door of the room where her other son lay dying, intent on keeping the young and healthy life from coming near. As he wandered through the damp heat that hung above the stream, Fabien fancied that he could still hear the sound of coughing.

A night came when he was awakened by the noise of ominous retchings. He heard a door creak, voices whispering, and the clink of china. He got up. The pitchpine of the stairs was cool to his bare feet. He crept to the closed door and caught from within the low murmur of frightened words: "Is it hopeless? Am I going to die?" and the voice of Madame Dézaymeries replying, "Yes, my boy, it is quite hopeless." "Have I still a month or two to live?" "No, Joseph, no." "A few weeks, then? . . ." Fabien put his hands over his ears, went back to his room, and stood leaning on the wooden balcony. The sound of living waters reached him. A dark blur of tree-tops half concealed the stars. A bird's note sounded like a sob.

During the days that followed, Madame Dézaymeries, as she ate her hurried meals, took note of Fabien's pallor. More than once she seemed to be on the point of issuing an order, but hesitated. At last she spoke. The doctors had said that he ought to go away at once. Joseph might linger on for months. It would be better for Fabien to return to Paris before the end of the holidays. He put up a show of resistance, but hoped that it would be overcome. At the end of August, since Joseph continued to enjoy an unhoped-for respite, he let himself be persuaded. He made use of his impending departure as an excuse for encouraging the dying boy. "D'you think I should be going away if there was really any danger?" But just as he was closing the door, the look of the lie fading from his face, he noticed in the glass of the wardrobe two eyes fixed upon him with lucid awareness, two agonized and dilated eyes that could read only too well the message of a face from which the mask had fallen. At that moment, though he had never been particularly fond of his brother, he recalled the games they had played together, and was assailed by a swarm of all the shared memories of their common childhood, of the pill-box in which they had kept their collection of pebbles, of the pine cone they had buried and dug up again when the next holidays came round. He wept because never again would he see this witness of his earliest years, this boy-priest with a heart devoured by love, who was more chaste than a young girl; this child who had been starved of all affection but had never uttered a word of complaint except to God.

3

JOSEPH DÉZAYMERIES died in the odor of sanctity on a day of early December. As soon as the funeral was over Fabien decided that he would stay with his mother until after the New Year holidays. Madame Dézaymeries allowed nothing, during those winter evenings, to distract her attention from the pale face of her surviving son. She noticed how, as Advent progressed, and already the appearance of Christmas trees and cradles kept the children's faces glued to the sweet-shop windows, he seemed to grow more tense and worried. She sat knitting garments for the poor. The sirens of ships leaving harbor, the rattle of cabs, the rustle made by the turning of a page, the chiming of clocks, some close at hand and others distant, the crackling of the fire—all these familiar, comfortable sounds had the effect of keeping Fabien uneasily on the alert. She looked at the young man facing her. Only in the dark, soft depths of his eyes could she still trace some remnant of the pious child he once had been. She prayed for Joseph, reciting in French the Canticle prescribed by the Church for use when interceding for the dead—"If Thou, Lord, shouldest mark iniquities, O Lord, who shall stand?" A deep despairing note crept into her voice which reminded Fabien of those days in his childhood when he had been taken to visit his father's grave in the country cemetery. On those occasions she had always told him to take off his cap. He had noticed the pathetic efforts made by the living to prevent the wild riot of nature, which crept up to the cemetery's very walls, from choking with grass and roots the space where the bodies which had given them life lay rotting in the ground. A damp wind was usually rattling the bleached and colorless beads of the funeral wreaths. . . . At other moments he saw again in memory the waxen mummy of his brother Joseph as it had lain upon the bed, the scalp showing white between the strands of hair, the bony structure of the face looking as though it were thrusting upward and about to pierce the skin's dry parchment. He sighed, and murmured: "Well, he is out of pain, now," to which she replied with relentless honesty, "Let us pray that he be out of pain."

On December 24th mother and son were sitting up preparatory to going to Midnight Mass. Between stars and roofs the chimes held sway.

Then Fanny came in.

They heard nothing, neither the sound of her cab, the ringing of the bell, nor the closing of the front door. She stood there, saying nothing, swathed in furs, a veil over her face. Only her painted mouth struck a vivid note. It was not smiling. For a moment or two she stayed where she was, not coming near them.

"Let me just look at you. . . . How you've grown, Fabien, how tall you are. . . ."

She stared at him as he moved away from the lamp. Then she said again: "Why, you're a man now!"

How was it that these perfectly ordinary and harmless words should sound so shameless? While she was speaking she had taken off her travelling hat, and now at last a smile showed in her rather shortsighted eyes. Nevertheless she seemed to diffuse an atmosphere of unease, of secretiveness. She talked of Joseph, mention of whose death she had seen in some newspaper. Fabien, struck dumb by emotion, kept his eyes fixed upon her. It was as though she had suddenly swum up from the depths of the last two years to the surface. He no longer recognized her. It was not that she looked older or more worn, but that she seemed to have become smaller, to have fallen away. The color of her hair was more violent than it used to be, her make-up cruder. Her body had thickened, and there was about it a sweet and heavy scent. Yes, her words were true. He had become a man, and that was why she frightened him.

All the same, he ran to the kitchen to make sure that Octavie was getting the green room ready. While he was gone, Fanny rather nervously explained the reason for her long silence.

"You look so stern, so hard!—much sterner and much harder than in the old days. I don't know how I'm going to be able to tell you. . . ."

Then, without any further beating about the bush, she announced that she was no longer living with her husband. They had been apart now for some considerable time.

"You've no idea, darling, what awful habits these sailors pick up!"

Thérèse never knew that Fanny had almost died of drug-poisoning when she was twenty. The wretched man she had married had turned her into an addict. She had to go into a home for treatment. . . . She stood, now, waiting for some word of compassion, some movement expressive of pity. But Madame Dézaymeries, rigid and silent, listened to her like a judge upon the bench. She was wearing a knitted cap of black

103

wool, and her neck was enclosed in a tight tulle collar with a white edging. Her thick eyebrows were twisted in a frown that gave her a hard expression. Her gray hair, drawn tightly back from the temples, gave the effect of having been flattened by the constant wearing of a nun's coif. Perhaps at that very moment Fanny may have been remembering the hot-tempered girl who, years ago, used to lecture her, and how the blood would suddenly rush into her colorless cheeks and flush them red: was seeing again the young rose-tree whose every bud had been cut and hoarded for the harvest of the Lord.

"I've divorced him," stammered Fanny. "I had every right to do so. I really think, Thérèse, that you are the only person in the whole world who would feel like this about it. Don't look so relentless. . . ."

Madame Dézaymeries remained icily aloof. The Irish woman, by this time thoroughly ill at ease, stood tidying her hair. She dared not look at her hostess, but almost in a whisper continued:

"What will you think when I tell you that I have married again? Is it a sin to want to be happy?"

Madame Dézaymeries silenced her with a gesture:

"That's enough! Say no more! I am not sitting in judgment on you, Fanny, but you must leave this house. For years I weakly listened to the promptings of my heart. I realize now the enormity of my crime. If I turn my back upon you it is not because of anything *I* feel. Another's safety is at stake, and for him I shall be held responsible through all eternity. . . . May mine be the guilt, and mine alone! . . . I beg you to forgive me. I shall never cease to pray for you, to suffer for you . . . but you *must* leave this house, Fanny!"

She opened the door, summoned Octavie, and told her to get the concierge to carry down the bags and call a cab.

"Are you really turning me out, Thérèse—*me*?" She began to sob, and Thérèse, looking at the features on which time had already left its traces, was reminded of the puckered face of a little girl in tears whom once she had comforted. She, too, was weeping, and could only repeat:

"I will pray for you: I will suffer for you!" She took the lamp, opened the door again, and stood waiting with lowered eyes.

It was at this moment that Fabien returned. He heard two voices speaking at the same time:

"You must say good-bye to her, my boy."

"Fabien, are you going to let her turn me out?"

Both women had expected the young man to show signs of amazement and despair. But he was perfectly calm. Nothing of the torment in his heart showed upon his face.

"What's the matter?" he asked.

"Would you believe it!" exclaimed Fanny, and her voice was hoarse. "Your poor mother's got to the point where she can't bear to have a divorced woman under her roof! . . . Really, that *is* a bit much!"

Madame Dézaymeries put a finger to her lips. Octavie had just come into the room to say that the bags had been brought down. Devoured by curiosity, alert to all that was going on, the old servant had left the door open and was hanging about the hall. Fabien, overcome by shyness, held out his hand to Fanny and withdrew it again rather too quickly. His eyes were dry. The traveller hurriedly fastened her coat and tied her veil. All she wanted now was to get away as soon as she could, away from Thérèse's pitiless face—away, especially, from the boy. What had his expression meant? Stupefaction or merely indifference? Indifference? Later that night, alone in her hotel bedroom, listening to the Christmas bells, she was to convince herself that his features, incapable of deception, had been eloquent, maybe of desire, but of repulsion, too, of disgust. At the moment of parting she could only blurt out:

"How I hate this religion of yours for coming between us. I would hate Him for coming between us—if He existed!"

She paused in the middle of her violent tirade, stretched her hands toward the door, and saw that Fabien was no longer there. His mother had told him to leave them, adding in a low voice:

"We shall not be going to Midnight Mass. We couldn't be in a proper state of mind after the horrible things that have been going on. Go to bed and forget what has happened."

Kneeling at her *prie-Dieu* with her face buried in her hands, she thrust her two thumbs into her ears that she might not hear the echo of that final blasphemy. Fanny gave one glance at the bent figure. Then, with one more insult, turned and left the room. For a moment she hesitated and sank down on the wood-chest in the hall. Within a cracked and frosted globe a gas-flame flickered. Then she got up and, without knocking, went into Fabien's room. A candle was burning on the night-table. The boy had sunk upon the bed, his face pressed into the pillow. At the sound of the door opening he turned his head and looked at her with sleepy eyes. Before he could do anything to defend himself, two hands had seized his face. He was conscious of a hesitating flutter of warm breath close to his lips, then, for a

106

brief moment, his mouth was caught and held before, with a sudden burst of laughter, she left him.

Standing by the rumpled bed he listened to that wild sound of mirth receding, but did not hear the slamming of the front door, nor yet the clatter of the departing cab, because the deep chime of the Cathedral bell was filling all the holy night.

He looked at his lips in the glass. He could taste on them the saltiness of blood.

4

HALF-NAKED though he was, he flung the window wide and breathed in the misty air. It was as though he took pleasure in feeling the sharp teeth and relentless violence of the December night. Leaning out above the street filled with its hubbub of footsteps and laughter, he shivered. He made, as might be, a sporting bet with himself to endure as long as he possibly could the death-grip of the winter darkness. Only these gulps of icy fog, he felt, could wash him clean again. He scrubbed at his lips with his bare arm. But even while he was conscious of a sense of disgust, of a longing to wipe away a stain, he felt that the beasts and gods patterned by the stars were the only worthy witnesses of a revelation the memory of which burned him more fiercely than the night air froze. He strained his body toward the sky. It was a vessel still stoppered and inviolate, but the kiss that had caught him on the brink of sleep had, though almost imperceptibly, cracked the seal.

Illness followed hard upon that night—an attack of pleurisy which made him free to partake of the glorious privileges accorded to those who are seriously sick, privileges that gave him the right to make no answer when he was spoken to; the right to sleep, or to pretend to sleep. He was blistered, and the pain revealed to him just how much agony the human body could endure. His mother being unable to stand the strain, a nun took over the nursing—a woman who was ageless, almost faceless, voiceless and anonymous. He revelled in the negative quality of her presence, in the crackling of her snow-white coif, in the sound made by her beads as she told them in the dark. One morning he looked in his mirror and saw the boyish fluff of beard, the large dark eyes such as the son raised from the dead must have fixed upon the widow of Nain. So rapid was his process of resurrection that in April he was passed fit for military service. It was not worth while to return to the École des Chartes for three months only, so he stayed with his mother, who was oppressed with a feeling of guilt in giving herself so completely to the pleasure of having him there.

To all appearances no memory of Fanny remained. All the same, neither mother nor son could any longer live as though a storm had not threshed the gray waters of their quiet existence. Thérèse Dézaymeries imposed upon herself a more exacting penance. As soon as she had heard early Mass she went to the hospital and tended the aged cancer patients—because only children appealed to her, and because no form of disease caused her such acute disgust as cancer. Their only visitors were the occasional begging Sisters who rang at the door of this dwelling which was always dark on the hottest days, because the blinds were kept carefully drawn in order to exclude the perilous gaiety of the light. Fabien would watch the play of dusty sunbeams on the moist surface of his hand and sit dreaming of the shrill cry of swifts or the throaty cooing of doves on hot tiles.

In July the Dézaymeries went back to the country, to a country buried in sand as in penitential ashes, with the stripped pines standing up like so many living examples of martyrdom humbly endured. Fabien, who wanted to do his service in the cavalry, spent his time riding over the sandy roads. A patch of fog would hide a stretch of grassland from view. Sheep would be indistinguishable from the mist. The night smell of the fens lasted on into the dawn. He made no effort to struggle against the torpor of his mind and heart. He surrendered to it. Wherever he went he carried with him the climate of his soul. As, when a child tormented by evil thoughts, he had closed his eyes and driven them away with a shake of the head, so now he forbad himself to look for Fanny in his heart. Later, thinking back to this period of his life, he was to feel amazement that he had been served so well by this curious mood of apathy. At the age when passions riot and flourish, he had been caught up into regions where the atmosphere was so rarefied that his desires, unable to breathe, had died. He scarcely fought against them at all, for there was no need for him to fight. His stainless life was no fruit of hard-won victory. He abandoned himself to a routine of piety which touched his sensibilities not at all, but was wholly mechanical. With childlike obedience he followed the path marked out for him.

So reassuring was his behavior that Madame Dézaymeries grew less watchful. She trusted him implicitly, and did not doubt that he had been signed, once for all, for salvation—that he was incorruptible. Perhaps, too, she was conscious of her powerlessness to break down the barrier of his silence and penetrate to the mind within. There was an unbridgeable gulf between them, each being of a different species, since each was of a different sex. But no matter how secret and puzzling the growth of the tree might be, she could see that it was beautiful. She could judge it by its fruit, and to her Christian heart the fruit was cause for rejoicing—for of what did it consist if not of spiritual humility, chastity, a willingness to work, and withdrawal from the world? How should she have realized that no love informed his attitude of submission? The spring of his nature had been coiled tight ever since his childhood days. It was to be expected that it should now show signs of slackening. But would not a day come when the solemn moments of the liturgical calendar would no longer find an echo in his heart? He might believe that he had banished Fanny from his mind, but in his flesh still lingered the memory of her fragrance, of the warmth of her breath. The expenditure of energy which he sought in his long rides through the woods was but the flight of Hippolytus wounded. The flies rose in a shimmer of sunlight from the peaty earth. They swarmed in a deadly cloud about his horse, making it sweat and bleed. He had to hurry home, and there, with his books, in the shuttered drawing room, wait for evening to bring respite. At dusk the smoke from the farmsteads and the burned-up grass spread over the fields of rye. He loved the fields when they were stitched with shadow. There had been, for as long as he could remember, a shortage of labor on the estate, and each year the forest had encroached a little further on the plow. The spaces of sky and open land grew ever narrower, and the dark ring drew tighter round the meadows. Perhaps, too, within himself the area of purity was insensibly contracting. But of this he was unaware, even during the years that he spent with the Dragoons at L. . . . The coarseness of his comrades alienated him by its very excess. He found nothing to attract him in the hotel bedrooms smelling of beeswax, leather and sweat, where a crowd of men and two women of the town sat pouring absinthe into the toilet jug. And, if his landlord's eldest daughter kept the vases in his room filled with

The Weakling and the Enemy

flowers, if she rose at dawn so that he might have a cup of steaming coffee before going on parade, if, one evening, wearing an imperfectly fastened dressing gown, she hung about tidying his cupboard, if on the day he left the town for good, her face showed red with crying as she said good-bye—these symptoms of desire and sorrow had no effect on him. He did not so much as turn his head as he rode away, did not so much as spare a glance for the heart which burned for love of him.

He returned to the heath country at the season when all work ceases, when the pines are left ungashed and no resin is collected because the wood pigeons are on the wing. Even the shepherds drive their flocks from their accustomed pastures lest the bleating and the trampling and the sound of sheep bells keep the shy birds from settling in the oaks.

On the first evening, Thérèse Dézaymeries took the bronzed face between her hands and looked long and hard into the eyes that made a show of smiling. But they quickly turned away. Dreams that she knew not of fought for concealment: desires lay hidden there like fish that darken the waters so that they may escape unseen. They took a turn together round the park. She did not ask him about his life in barracks, nor had he anything to tell her. They walked with their heads thrown back. Dreamily she murmured words that she loved to speak on their country strolls: "Pine forests—the only forests in which one can see the sky!" . . . and, indeed, above their heads the tree-tops formed a vast tattered and swaying curtain through the holes in which they could catch sight of small patches of dark and shimmering blue. Mist rose from the stream and eddied about the fields through which it ambled lovingly, and the scent of wild mint struck through the wreathing vapor more powerfully than the smell of briars and resin and bruised leaves. Thérèse Dézaymeries thought that Fabien's melancholy was but the brooding of a mind which finds God in the onset of the night. Next day he refused to go pigeon-shooting. He grumbled because the presence of the guns made riding impossible. Perhaps because he was unaided now by the terrific physical fatigue which had been his constant companion when in barracks, he turned in on himself, seeking an identity he could not find. The gestures and the prayers of former days seemed like the gestures and the prayers of someone else. The habits of body and mind which belonged to a youth that was his no longer he strove to force upon the stranger who now lived within him, a stranger to be dreaded, on whom he gazed with fear. He began to be conscious of an inner emptiness, or rather, of a feeling that he had been abandoned. And that, in itself, was a form of faith, because one cannot be abandoned except by somebody.

His mother hung about him continually, scanning his face, repressing certain thoughts that rose in her about his life at L. . . .

She wrote to her Spiritual Director:

"When he was a small boy I had only to take him on my knee. Not that he at once revealed the reason for his melancholy, but he was willing that I should probe his heart. He helped me in my search, and, when I had found the hidden thorn that irked him, ran away comforted. But he no longer believes that the old woman who bore him and nourished him, and gave him a second birth into the life of grace, can any longer supply the healing balm. Should I, do you think, ask more people to the house? There are several families in the neighborhood of more or less our own social standing, families with young girls. I don't want to, but I will if you say so. I remember reading in Pascal that marriage is the lowest of all Christian states, vile and unpleasing to God. How strongly I feel the truth of that! How convinced I am that the traffic of the flesh is a grim and filthy business. I long to say so to my child, who as yet, I am ready to swear, knows nothing of it. I sometimes wonder whether the passage through his life of that woman whose name I never mention has not, perhaps, left traces of trouble in his heart. His silence on the subject is far from reassuring. . . ."

The good Father advised that she should wait and watch: that she should be in no hurry to point the way to marriage (though it was very reprehensible on her part to espouse the derogatory views of a heretic on that great Sacrament). It was important to make quite certain, first of all, that Fabien had not been called to a higher destiny. "It might, perhaps, be no bad thing if the dear lad travelled for a while. Let him go to Umbria, to Rome especially. Those places will divert his thoughts, but piously. They may even bring him back by pleasant by-ways to that state of mind in which you, no less than I, desire to see him anchored."

When first she made the suggestion, and as she uttered the one word "Italy," Fabien felt the stranger lurking within him tremble with joy. With the same determination she had shown when formerly she had insisted on his settling in Paris, the good woman now pushed open the double door of this mysterious room. Pious hands drew him from the darkness and thrust him sharply into the arena where the fierce sun beats, and ever hungry beasts prowl up and down.

5

UMBRIA disappointed Fabian. The Christ of St. Damian who spoke to Il Poverello had no message for him. The sleeping face of St. Clare, and the veiled member of her Sisterhood who watched over her, did not stir his sleeping heart. Joyless, he tramped the road from Perugia to Spoleto by way of Assisi and Foligno, deaf to the fiery Canticle addressed by Umbria to her brother the Sun. For him the dust of these highways held no trace of Francis, nor yet of Brother Leo, the little lamb of God. Why did he decide to make his way, not to Rome where he longed to be, but to Venice? Not chance, he thought, decides these things. Someone there must be who sets in motion the impulse buried deep within us. Another climate beckoned him. Until the moment of this journey the young man, unresponsive though he might be to the Holy Spirit, had at least been aware of Its presence. For years no inner tide had carried Fabien on its bosom: but he knew that He who did not draw him to Himself existed. In Venice this child of the Christian tradition was made for the first time aware of his lack of grace. He was alone. The sense of an infinite emptiness was revealed to him. His heart swelled. He knew the treacherous delights that are the mark of that terrible withdrawal. Abandoning his books and notes he wandered, unseeing, from museum to museum. He had no eyes for the sleeping St. Ursula as painted by Carpaccio, for the unsullied breeze that fills her room of slumber, for the day open on the darkness, for the angel who leaves untouched the things of every day—slippers, lamp, crown and the half-read page. He preferred the network of evil-smelling lanes, and, at dusk, those districts where languid voices whispered of proffered pleasures. The shoddy music of gay orchestras floating at night upon the Grand Canal in a mist of lanterns brought tears to his eyes. God had departed from him, though not yet did he know the true meaning of solitude. He was like a frightened child whose father has let go his hand. He was fearful at being thus abandoned, yet revelled in his fear. A sense of pleasure caught him by the throat because, for the first time, he knew that he was vulnerable. To see himself exposed, like a virgin to the ravening beasts, was already a delight. He knew that sin, mortal sin, might pounce upon him now from the concealing thickets, and drive straight to his undefended heart. He turned his eyes upon the stranger that was himself, this new, this unsuspected being, whom Evil might possess. His defenses were down. Nothing now stood between his fainting spirit and the vast abyss. He had a feeling of giddiness, and found in his awareness of it ecstatic pleasure. He would not go out of his way to provoke attack, he would take no chances. It was enough for him—a proffered victim, a willing prey—to taste the joy of expectation long drawn out. On the ferry-boats, at Florian's, in his hotel that looked on the Salute, the facile fumes of Asti kept the charm alive. Formerly, like all those whose thoughts are centered on the dialectic of the soul, he had been incapable of seeing anything save through mists engendered by a ceaseless meditation. Venice had the effect of dispelling the cloud. She laid her hand upon him, and his eyes were opened. For the first time faces stood out from the featureless mass around him. He saw them and he loved them. He was conscious, too, that his own face had become the focus for passing glances.

One evening, in the dining-room of his hotel, he felt irked by the fact that someone he did not know was staring at him. The importunate stranger was a big, sturdily-built man with prominent eyes of china-blue. He had the sparse fair hair and ruddy complexion of the north, the full-blooded cheeks produced by mists and alcohol. Facing him, with her back to Fabien, was a woman, and on his right sat a very young man who talked a lot and waved his arms. So high-pitched was his voice that, but for the gipsy band, Fabien could easily have heard what he was saying. He was not addressing his remarks to the woman at his side, who, with back bent, shoulders hunched, and her elbows on the table, gave the effect of someone loosely sprawling. His thick black hair fitted close above his eyebrows like a cap. He had thick lips, and the blueness of his jowl was evidence of an exuberant growth of beard with which his razor fought a losing battle. He had quite forgotten to eat, and the gravy on his plate was fast congealing. He took some paper and a fountain pen from his pocket and started to draw, making some remark as he did so that brought a smile to the lips of his red-faced companion. At that moment the waiter made as though to clear the table, and at once the young man flung himself upon the food before him and cleared his plate with the swiftness of a famished dog.

At length the three of them rose. The elder man, as soon as he got up, was seen to be a veritable giant. He might have been a Prince of some Scandinavian Royal House. The youth, whose length of body from shoulder to waist had, while he was sitting, given the impression that he was of about the same height, reached scarcely to his shoulder. Fabien had never seen anyone quite like him. He wore very tight trousers of light-colored cloth which accentuated the abnormal development of his thighs, which might have been those of an acrobat. He made no attempt to give the woman precedence, but, with an air of cool insolence and a toothpick jutting from his mouth, made for the door, followed by the rubicund giant who once more stared at Fabien as he passed his table. Their companion stayed behind to drink a glass of water, and Fabien, who ever since the beginning of the meal had been eager to see her face, watched her intently. At last she turned round, and he recognized Fanny.

Only a paradox can express his feelings at that moment. He recognized her *although* she had not changed. The modern miracle which has given to women the seeming boon of eternal youth produces in some people, of whom Fabien Dézaymeries was one, a sense of terror and disgust. In these young women of fifty, preserved by some supernatural agency, the eyes alone are eloquent of age. Only in them can be read the secret of a flabbiness that has its origin in the soul; only through them is made visible the wear and tear of the spirit. Fanny had remained so much the same that the effect was frightening. She looked as she had always looked, though the flood of time had swept her on, and each passing moment had marked her as with fire: five years of exigent desires and glutted senses, of lovers lost and lovers found, of passionate abandonments and bleak awakenings: five years of late nights, of endless cigarettes, of rich food, strong drink, narcotics and drugs. Yet there she stood, her young body apparently untouched by the passing of the years, strong as steel, tempered and hardened and possessed.

The Weakling and the Enemy

Sin, in its way, is a form of life. There is such a thing as *infernal* grace, and it can galvanize, just for as long as may be necessary, that adorable shape of molded flesh which, according to St. Catherine of Siena, stinks in all its parts.

She filled her glass with water, sipped slowly until she had emptied it, took her bag which was hanging on the chair, and brushed by the young man without seeing him. She was wearing a dress of rose-colored brocade cut in the prevailing Poiret fashion, and Turkish slippers slightly turned up at the toes. Her fragrance struck at Fabien, nor could he be sure whether it came from her body or from the long dead days that she had made to live again. He followed her into the hall. She was engaged in a lively discussion—though she kept her voice low—with the elder of the two men (no doubt, her second husband), whose ham-like face was distended in a grin. Meanwhile, the strange-looking youth, now wearing a felt hat and carrying a light overcoat on his arm and an ivory-knobbed cane in his hand, was giving instructions to the porter about forwarding his letters. He lit a cigarette, and then, presumably because the discussion was going on longer than he liked, said:

"Are your bags ready, Donald?"

The other man kissed Fanny's hand and went over to his companion. She remained standing where she was, struck rigid, it seemed, with amazement, and with her eyes fixed on the revolving door. Fabien was gently swaying in a rocking chair, but he finished his cigarette in a couple of minutes. He felt, from the way in which Fanny's two partners were casting sidelong glances at him, that he had been the subject of the recent conversation. He had no doubt at all that they had been talking of him. The younger of the two appeared to be countering some angry remark made to him by the red-faced man, who finally went up to Fanny again and asked her to go with him, for a moment, to his room. Without saying a word, she followed him to the lift. The youth called after them:

"Don't forget, Donald: we ought to leave here not later than a quarter past ten. The train goes at twenty to."

Donald nodded. His smile of assumed candor was horrible. He made a furtive movement of the hand in Fabien's direction.

Scarcely had the couple vanished from sight than the young man approached Fabien in a rather secretive manner and asked him for a light. As a cockchafer agitates its wing-cases preparatory to taking flight, he showed in a number of ways that he wanted to begin a conversation.

"It's really very hard, terrible, actually," he began at last, "to have to leave Venice in the autumn" (he spoke in a singsong, and his r's rattled like a fall of pebbles). "No one ever *leaves* Venice, you know: they *tear* themselves away. To be in Venice is to live in an *embrace*."

Fabien smiled but said nothing. The other went on: "Don't you think so, *actually*? It certainly is so in my case, but perhaps you are here alone?"

Fabien felt obliged to nod. The creature before him assumed an air of disapproval and pity.

"Oh, but how *imprudent*! Alone in Venice! The Goddess of Love will punish you! To be alone in Venice is like—if you will excuse the simile—indulging in solitary vice!"

Fabien condescended neither to smile nor to make the slightest gesture. But the stranger obviously interpreted his silence as evidence of interest, for he pointed with his cane at the revolving door.

The Weakling and the Enemy

"Over there stands the witness of many quite *terribly* sad deaths—I mean the Salute. *Actually,* no one could *possibly* reckon up all the young people who have drowned themselves from its steps. One of them was a *great* friend of mine—perhaps you have read some of his poetry?—just a *leetle* bit old-fashioned in manner, perhaps one might almost say *passé,* but then he was only seventeen, you see, and was quite unacquainted with modern art—all the same, he was a god, *actually.* It was the year I was dancing at the Fenice. . . ."

Fabien stared with amazement at this youth with the over-developed thighs. So that was it: he was a dancer! But still he said nothing. The stranger, after a quick glance at his wrist watch, hurried on:

"I'm afraid my mind was wandering. You see, before I go I want to ask you whether you would take on a little mission—actually, that is just the word for it—something that will add a charming note of romance, a delightful *soupçon* of sentiment to your stay here. I won't ask whether you know me: I have, alas! to forego the pleasures of anonymity. They have become quite impossible since the magazines of two hemispheres have taken to printing my portraits. . . ."

Fabien replied dryly that he never looked at magazines.

"But my dear sir, do you mean, *actually,* that you have never seen a picture of Cyrus Bargues?"

Fabien remembered that he had seen the name on some poster or other advertising a season of exotic ballets. The dancer was staring at the imbecile who did not even know who he was!

"If you are not interested in art I very much doubt whether you will consent to undertake this mission which, on the strength of a first favorable impression, I had quite made up my mind to offer you. Your eyes, as you must often have been told, are quite *unique."*

Clearly, he must be a specialist in the matter of eyes, and probably knew all about them as a collector knows all about, say, medals. The fire that glowed deep down in Fabien's held his attention so completely that he looked at least ten times at his wrist watch without seeming to take in at all what its message was. But it was true that he was in a hurry. How could he manage, in the space of a few minutes, to convince this handsome, silent barbarian? Awkwardly, in a torrent of words, he delivered himself of the errand with which he had been entrusted.

"Donald Larsen, my impresario—yes, the tall man with the fair hair—has to go to Switzerland to make final arrangements about Leda Southers' engagement. . . ."

"Leda Southers?"

So, actually, he'd never heard of Leda Southers! Why, with Leda and Cyrus Bargues what more could Larsen possibly ask for? He would have the finest ballet company in the world!

"Don't you understand, it will be *immense,* there's no other word for it. . . . But, unfortunately, there is a woman in Donald's life—his wife, yes, the woman who was here a moment ago. . . ."

Again he looked at his wrist watch, hesitated for a brief moment, looked at Fabien, saw that he was now eagerly listening, and grew bolder:

"D'you know, she followed us to Venice—we couldn't stop her—*actually* on the ground that Leda Southers had once been Donald's mistress!"

The trouble, he said, about Donald was that he wasn't ruthless enough. One couldn't cure him of being *sorry* for people. "She keeps her hold on him by threatening to commit suicide. But I *did* get him to promise that he wouldn't take her to Switzerland with us. She keeps on saying that she'll kill herself —and he says she's quite capable of doing it. Personally, I make a point of pretending not to believe her. What *I* happen to know, though Donald doesn't, is that Fanny had arranged to meet a gigolo here—but he hasn't turned up. If only he'd come she'd be willing enough to leave us alone. . . . I think, perhaps, I ought to explain that she *did* try to kill herself once, in Paris, but she didn't bring it off. . . ."

"Why are you telling me all these excessively grubby details?"

"You don't appear to be altogether indifferent to them."

Fabien got up, threw away the cigarette which he had only just lighted, took a few paces, and came back to his companion. He muttered, as though talking to himself, "So she tried to kill herself, did she?" So upset was he by what he had just heard that he was no longer listening to the dancer who seemed to be completely overcome by the rapid success that had attended his efforts.

"If I were the *patron,*" he went on, "there wouldn't be all this shilly-shallying. After all, what *is* a woman, actually, I mean? One woman more or less in the world can't *really* matter, can it? I wish I could make you see how tremendously important this Swiss trip is. A ballet—how shall I put it?—a sort of cosmic, a sort of *geological,* ballet—which will express the awakening of primeval forces, the primitive *spark,* the first *distension* of matter by the impact of life."

His large nose twitched, his thick lips parted, so that his mouth looked like a bleeding gash in the rind of a ripe fruit.

123

But Fabien had thoughts only for the great wind that had transported him far from the remote corner of heath and pine, from the desert in which he had been born, to this coast where Fanny, old now and soiled by life, had looked for death—for eternal death. . . . Surely it could be no chance meeting? Must he, then, risk damnation that she might be saved? No . . . no. . . . It was no longer a matter of flesh and grace in conflict. The two all-powerful forces would work, now, in close alliance for the salvation of a woman's body, a woman's soul.

"So now, my dear sir, you know that there is in this hotel a lonely woman whom I may, perhaps, be allowed to describe as a professional suicide. Let me repeat what I have told you once already—that she has made one attempt, and failed. It is madness on our part to throw her at your head like this, but we have no alternative—you do realize that, don't you? Maybe you like women of her peculiar type? You can save her at very small cost to yourself. All you have to do is to hand her back to Donald when he returns. He doesn't *want* to lose her, you know. She's got—how shall I put it—a wonderful nose for picking up a good thing, for finding budding geniuses. You should see the pictures and the lacquer she's got in Paris."

He took Fabien's arm and gave it a farewell squeeze. But Fabien stood perfectly still, gazing at the lift.

"There she is . . . promise me . . ."

With the faintest flicker of his eyelids Fabien conveyed consent. The bellboy emerged with the bags, followed by Larsen, who, in his travelling ulster with its fur collar, looked larger than ever. Fanny brought up the rear. While Cyrus Bargues was speaking in a low voice to the impresario, the latter kept his eyes fixed on Fabien. The giant paused for a moment in the door of the hotel, turned once more to Fanny and wagged his finger, as one might do to a child when conveying a parting "Be good." For the last time he shot a brooding look at Fabien; for the last time the little dancer grinned. . . . Then Fabien, conscious that there was nothing now to restrain him, went across to the woman who was still standing motionless, gazing at the door, touched her on the shoulder, and said quite simply:

"Fanny!"

6

FOR a second or two she failed to recognize him; then she uttered a faint cry:

"You! . . . here in Venice, you, Fabien!"

She raised her face to his, careless of the danger she ran in thus displaying its mask of paint and powder in the harsh light of the hotel hall. But tears had seamed the mask and broken its surface. Suddenly her gaze expressed nothing but the dull amazement of a woman brought in an instant face to face with a miracle, not believing what she sees before her, denying the evidence of her own eyes.

"You here . . . You here!"

Hurriedly he began to speak of his mother, of Joseph, striving to build up a façade of meaningless detail. She only said again, "You here!" She had been on the point of dying from starvation, and here, suddenly, was this large, warm loaf within reach of her hand, within reach of her mouth. Just as the anchor had been raised, the last mooring-rope loosened; just as the ship was beginning to move out to the dim, dark distance, he who was the furthest from her in space and time, he, this great archangel, had turned up beside her.

She glanced round the hall. Yes, she was really awake. Two porters were quarrelling over a tip. Some Americans were talking with a nasal twang that made them sound like gramophone records.

"Come with me . . . away from this light . . . come!"

The Weakling and the Enemy

She had thrown a coat over her shoulders and now moved
away, drawing Fabien after her. The grip of her hand on his
arm was that of a drowning woman. The mingled smell of
ooze and musk, the confused odors of scented cigarettes and
marshland, the wavering reflections of green and red cast by the
lanterns in the dark water—all these things that, but a moment
before, had seemed the forerunners of death, now suddenly and
forever became part and parcel of her frantic joy. This harbor
whence ships sailed out into the great nothingness had, in a
moment, taken on the appearance of some brightly lit scene set
for the action of her happiness. She understood nothing of the
broken, stammered phrases in which Fabien was taking terrified refuge from the threat of silence. She had ears only for his
voice, for the fresh, male voice of this child-man, and hugged it
to her heart.

They crossed the Piazetta and walked along the quays. They
had to take very short steps because of the narrow skirt of her
brocaded dress. And what of him? He knew that now at last he
had stepped across the forbidden threshold. After all these years,
here he was on the other side—but whether dead or alive he did
not know. What was this happiness the mere approach of which
set his heart swelling and transfigured all the world around
him?

"Fanny, what has happened to you?"

Such was the first tiny phrase he uttered in the language of this
unknown land into which he was striding so incautiously. It
was Fanny now who was talking, he who, without understanding what he heard, was listening to her rather throaty
voice. She was confessing that someone she had thought to be
her friend, someone to whom she had cried aloud in her dis-

tress, had not come. But how sweet now seemed that treachery, how sincerely she rejoiced in the thought of that abandonment! Now and again she stopped in the middle of her flow of words.

"How can I dare to say all this to you who are so innocent?"

He was still for her the Fabien Dézaymeries whom she had known of old—the simple, unspoiled schoolboy. She had opened the lovely book at the page she had been reading when she closed it. The old frank laugh rang out again for a moment as she said:

"Are you still as religious as ever? This meeting has altered my views of Providence."

Unknown to her the fruit had been ripening just when the pangs of thirst were most intense. Something told her that this soul was utterly defenseless—that at the very first assault she could possess it. The young victim lay trembling beneath her hand, unarmed, with no power to resist, already drunk with the fumes of defeat. Time, in her absence, had brought to maturity the seed that she had sown within his heart, and now she had returned at the very moment of harvest.

Standing beneath a street lamp, she opened her black silk bag. Fabien saw the glint of a tiny revolver.

"You are the only person in the world who could have held me back from the last fatal leap—the only one, and you were so far away. And now you're here, you're here!"

Her hand touched his hair, stroked the rough surface of his cheeks. Using a shop window as a mirror, she powdered her face and reddened her lips, like an actress putting a few finishing touches to her make-up before going back upon the stage. Then, in the narrow entry of a deserted café, she clung to Fabien, burying her face in his shoulder as might a child who has found sudden respite from its misery. He noticed then that the cheeks of women who have been crying have the smell of wet earth.

She laughed, and her voice was bruised by the violence of the sobs she had been choking back. Once more she took him in her arms. Thus did she wreak her vengeance on Thérèse Dézaymeries! Driven from her friend's house, she had crept back by way of Fabien's heart. Soon she would dominate his body, too. If only Thérèse could have seen them! She laughed through her tears. Not yet was she quite ripe for death. Once more she would see the morning sun drench with flame the tumbled bed. The fledgling she had hatched, the young creature who for her alone had grown to manhood, trembled.

To them, snared in the enchantments of the body, the echoes of the city's life reached as a medley of mere sound, void and meaningless: music and the sound of laughter, footsteps on the flagstones of the quay, the plash of wavelets and the susurration of ships' prows cleaving the waters of the lagoon. Deeper and deeper did Fabien drive his way into the revealing night—from evening until dawn, and through the day that followed it, a day of rain when the hotel was filled with the whisper of steps in every corridor and the muted playing of an orchestra. Beneath the stirring of his breath a woman was coming back to life. She said to him:

"I hang upon your breath. . . ."

Tomorrow, doubtless, the time would come to make a reckoning. Tomorrow he must descend into the arena and count the bodies of the slain. He must measure the extent of harvest fields flattened by this storm of hail, calculate the miles of virgin forest burned to ashes by this fire.

The Weakling and the Enemy

At length, but half alive, they left the room, and Atilio, the gondolier, steered them, as the whim took him, by the rioting green of walls from which the autumn leaves were falling. At the hour of the siesta they landed on the island of San Francesco-del-Deserto. A friar, his eyes puffy with sleep, half opened the wicket gate, and they caught a glimpse of cloisters, of a well-head, and, against the dazzling blue, of a single cypress. Then the door was closed against the guilty couple. The clack of sandals died away and was lost in the silence of drowsiness and prayer. On another occasion a flicker of flames lit up for them the golden glints within the dark basilica of Padua, where, to a murmured hymn, the monks were bearing in procession a great bleeding Christ. On the empty Lido sands innumerable bathing huts drawn up in rows told more surely of approaching winter than did the arrow-shaped flight of birds migrating. From all the campaniles sounded the evening prayer for grace, and from an acquiescent sky there fell an absolution on the fleet of gondolas and all their loads of sin. Fabien, erect at the center of this burning, fiery furnace, knew that behind them a threat of storm was mounting, accumulating all the arrears of a fearful debt. Without a halt, without so much as pausing to take breath, he was descending an endless flight of stairs in a giddiness of lusts repeatedly renewed, of rending sensations, of the gloomy stupor of satiety. But had he ever imagined, for a moment, what he would find at the bottom of that long descent? Suddenly the rain had come, transforming Venice to a great mist of moisture. The radiators gurgled and gave out a smell of hot painted metal that filled the room's disorder of woman's clothes and books and bottles. Watchful and experienced, Fanny looked for the first signs of weariness upon the thin-drawn face, beneath the

130

mournful eyes. She began to talk about going home. Fabien was like a man waking from a heavy sleep. The course of the descent was broken, and, on the landing where he rested, he knew that Someone waited. For years he had lived a life of chastity and religious devotion, feeling that presence only as something still far off. But now, after a strange and errant course, after treading the winding ways of an exquisite guilt, he felt upon his face the very breeze and breath of condemnation.

But it was on the journey home, especially, imprisoned in their sleeper where he had to submit to the experience of feeling shut in, of knowing that he could not get away, that he realized with astonishment how strangely his long fall had ended. The pleasures of the flesh that blunt so many hearts, had restored to his a mystic sensibility. His mistress was there with him in all the vulnerable intimacy of proximity. Never had they spent so long a time together, never had they seen one another so clearly, as during those long and gloomy hours between Venice and Paris. For hitherto their love had been a bird of darkness. Deep in himself, but very far removed, he felt the presence of that Being whom he had betrayed—while here, within touching distance of his hand, within the very radius of his breathing, was, all the while, this aging partner of his sin. The further the train travelled from the sun, the heavier lay the autumn's wounding hand upon the forests. Great flocks of crows swooped down upon the stubble fields. Fanny was smiling at the thought of winter now close at hand—of that season when lovers in the languor of their satisfied desires hear the patter of drops upon the windows, the sighing of the wind, when, deep in a room drowned in the Paris rain, the clock ticks on its empty reckoning of a life where time means nothing.

The Weakling and the Enemy

In the dining-car she discussed practical details. Fabien must move from his hotel. She knew of a ground-floor flat in the rue Visconti. Would he let her furnish it for him? Everyone in Paris admitted that she had a "gift" for that sort of thing. And it would really be doing her a service; she had a perfect mania for picking up bargains.

"I don't know where to put all the stuff I've got."

Her dear, scatter-brained darling, for whom the outside world scarcely existed, wouldn't, would he—she asked—mind if now and then a chair was spirited away? There are some things one keeps for years, others that one gets rid of in a week.

But Fabien was not listening. His whole mind was bent on the idea of escape.

"You'll come and see me often, won't you? What a sensation you'll be, my tiger-cat! You care so little about art, and certainly Thérèse was the last person in the world capable of teaching you to appreciate beautiful things. She's always had an instinctive love of the ugly. But then, of course, ugliness is a matter of principle with her. I know you're intelligent, but not in matters of that kind."

He broke in on her talk with a harsh gesture, furious that she should have dared to speak of Madame Dézaymeries. She fell silent, quick to notice the dark mood that cast a shadow on her loved one's face. She was no longer intent on changing Fabien. Her knowledge of men made her realize that he would be quite unresponsive to any such attempt. It was simply a question for her of taking him as he was, of drawing him to her with all his heavy load of torment, credulity and remorse. In their early days together she had tried to win him by pretending to be attracted by his metaphysical dreaming. But he had eluded her every attempt to broach the subject. It was as though he had a horror of hearing words he held sacred spoken by lips like hers. Within the little mahogany box of their sleeper Fanny set herself to read the formidable language of his face, to interpret the meaning of his every silence. She guessed that he was longing to escape, and trembled when she heard his somewhat theatrical reply to what she had just been saying:

"There will be no place for me in your house. Do you really think that I am prepared to accept every extreme of marital forbearance?"

With his mind on Donald Larsen he added: "From now on he is a co-conspirator with us."

With a gesture that she knew well, of the meaning of which she was only too conscious, he buried his face in his hands. She was caught by sudden panic. Tomorrow morning, in the shoddy dawn of the Gare de Lyons, would she not see him vanish, disappear forever? Had the time come to play her last card, that threat of suicide which still worked with her wretched husband? She had no idea how a young Christian would react to it, so unfamiliar was she with the type. Might it not be that he would accept his mistress' damnation with a light heart?

A railway official entered to prepare their beds and dim the light. Fabien sought the solitude of the corridor, where he stood with his forehead pressed to the rain-drenched window. A few paces off, Fanny watched him. Tonight the noise made by the train as it rushed through unknown stations struck a note of torment to the very heart of their love-making. It was as though, in a desperate heroism, they had mingled their bodies on the edge of an eternal nothingness.

133

7

FANNY had to play her hand, at first, very carefully. The young man, ever ready to take fright, refused absolutely to live anywhere but in the hotel in the rue de Vaugirard to which he had grown accustomed. Every other day he met his mistress in a ground-floor flat in the rue Visconti, where the only permanent piece of furniture seemed to be the divan bed, where the chairs and screens that stood about the room changed continually. From each of these trysts he emerged so exhausted, so melancholy and so resentful, that she was left with a feeling that she would never see him again. But always he was the first to arrive, impatient to perform the act for which he had come. From this she drew no favorable omen: "He enjoys it, that's perfectly clear . . . but the chief reason is that he fears I will kill myself if he plays me false." She was forever alluding to the possibility of her death: the subject, in fact, had become a perfect mania with her, and the glint of the revolver still showed whenever she opened her bag. It wasn't that she wanted to exert any kind of emotional blackmail on him, but that, as she confessed, nothing gave her such a thrill as the feeling that she was all the time playing a dangerous game with fate.

"I used to be a terrible gambler, darling; but what's money, after all? What I need today is the knowledge that the stake is living flesh and blood, that I'm playing for *you*! I've put everything on you, and, when all's said and done, it's only my own life that's in the balance."

She had as yet ventured to invite him to the Quai Debilly, though she would never really be at rest until he was breathing the air that she habitually breathed, until she could feel that he was continually within her reach. How happy, therefore, it made her to discover that the thought of her unknown life apart from him caused him acute suffering—that he was actually jealous of the woman from whom he longed to be delivered. To his first clumsy questionings she replied quite simply that her life was an open book:

"When you see the kind of people, my dear, among whom I spend my time, you'll stop worrying. Artists are all very well for casual conversation or business deals, but when it comes to love! . . ."

Fabien emitted one of those bursts of frank laughter which he never, except on rare occasions, succeeded in controlling. They always gave the impression that some vast reserve of youth and happiness within him had come suddenly to the boil.

At first he hovered uncertainly upon the frontiers of her strange kingdom, fearful, as in his native heaths, of venturing on to squelching bogs. Nothing that he now did showed any eagerness to escape. The trapped animal, after his first violent struggles, has a way of staying motionless for so long that he produces the illusion of death. Knowledgeable and patient, she had finally succeeded in enveloping him completely. In his moments of satiety he thought: "I'll run away from all this grubby playing ground, from all this filth of mind and body"; but then desire would stir in him again. At Fanny's parties he was most commonly to be seen leaning against a doorway and saying nothing. The other guests were as strange to him as the members of some savage tribe. He wandered among them, a melancholy Gulliver, the prisoner of an unknown race. The talk was all of the impending return of Donald Larsen and of Cyrus Bargues, who was at present dancing in London. He was bewildered by the incomprehensible pictures on the walls, and by the music, which sounded to him like recurrent blows with a fist. There was no sign of servants, and at supper-time the guests helped themselves. Under the influence of drink masks did, to some extent fall, but there was always one still clamped to each face. Had he been able to tear it away what raw wound would have been revealed? What was this leprosy he could not see though it stank in his nostrils? At first he felt humiliated when he heard for the first time the name of some musician who was, according to Fanny, the most renowned in Europe, of some poet, of some collector. He suffered agonies when his was the only solemn face while all around the company was doubled up with mirth. . . . But the jokes were all about people he did not know, and the jargon, with its indirect references and implications, was like a foreign language to him. This was a world of which his intelligence had not the freedom. He stood in it like a blind man at a fireworks display. He could hear the "Ah's" of the crowd, the banging of the rockets, but not a glimmer of light reached him through the darkness.

These Philistines had begun by laughing at him, as at some Samson cropped and weaponless. In confidential whispers and at a safe distance (for he looked a tough customer) they exchanged pleasantries on the subject of his presence there among them. But of all this he seemed to be completely unaware, seemed not even to notice how the women sniffed round his body. In the noisy din of the supper table he had ears only for the soughing of his native forests under an autumn rain. The air might be shrill with the voices of ageless women in backless dresses, but what he heard was the sound of pigeons swooping to roost among the oaks. He could catch the wildness of the wind driving the rain against the windows of the nursery where his brother had breathed his last. From far back (and herein lay the secret of his taciturnity) he had, though he did not know it, been oppressed by a grievance against his mother caused by her inflexible austerity, and unconsciously he accused her of painting the world black and showing life in nothing but gloomy colors. But he knew now that the world is a place of leprosy, that life is the home of death. He could see, he could feel, the canker at the hearts of all these people. He was terrified by the stench of his own rottenness. It was true, perhaps, that his mother, under the influence of her own Jansenist upbringing and of a slightly warped vision, had been guilty of distorting the doctrines of her faith: yet, compared with what he saw about him, how right she had been! Though he might entirely fail to understand the poetry, the painting, the music which those around him seemed to admire so much, he could not help feeling that the men responsible for these things had, maybe, employed their art in the creation of a universe of monsters with the object of being able to move among them unnoticed. Was it not true to say, he thought, that their art was the visible form of their despair?

Why, then, did he not profit from the violent shock administered to him by this backfiring of sin? Why, then, wakened by the thud of his fall, did he not take to his heels? If only he could turn to account the sense of horror that pressed so close upon satiety. . . . But Fanny would kill herself. He alone it was who stood between her and the abyss: he was her sole defense against that will to death which kept on coming to the surface of her mind. There were moments when he felt ashamed of his secret wish that she would act upon it. If only she would get out of his life, if only she would vanish forever, if only this torment of his existence would cease, leaving him like a garden with a fresh patina of green after the hail had passed! Why should the weary be refused the boon of sleep? But he did not believe that death was sleep. He believed only in an eternity of rest or punishment—in an ineffable Presence forever there, or forever absent. He believed that absence and presence are the two contrasted aspects of eternity—that there is no third possibility, no refuge for those who, having been the enemies of God and man alike, long only for the dark and nothingness.

8

IN THE rainy dawn, as he stood waiting for the door to be opened, Fabien saw, on the pavement opposite, a number of shadowy figures pass one by one through the half-opened wicket of the Carmelite Chapel where the bell was calling to early Mass. He dreaded lest one of them should turn its head and, with face suddenly displayed, smile with his mother's eyes and lips. He climbed his staircase, which was misted with the stale smell of yesterday's food. The shoes standing outside the doors told mute stories of laborious lives. A telegram was lying on his table. Just as he was about to open it, he remembered that it was the anniversary of Joseph's death.

Memorial service for Joseph Thursday ten o'clock. Expecting you.

He must get off at once, before he might have to fight his way through Fanny's entreaties! Hurriedly he packed a bag and scribbled a note for his mistress. Might not this be the prelude to final and permanent escape? Here was one of those chances that he could not possibly have engineered. His own choice, his own will, had had nothing whatever to do with it. Someone was taking a hand in his life. Someone, perhaps, was concerned about his destiny. It was beyond his power *not* to take the train, *not* to feel his mother's arms about him, *not* to press with his knees the oblong of sand under which his brother slept, *not* to plunge into that atmosphere which death creates, with which he had always tended, since the days of his childhood, to saturate his mind. He began to suffer when, with nothing left to do, he sat waiting in his room until it should be time to start for the station. Suddenly he felt that he would like to say a prayer for the dead boy. Between his brother and himself there lay a solid block of sin—no life-giving corn crop but a foul, luxuriant weed. He could, of course, still pray, but of what avail were prayers uttered from such unholy depths? With the tears streaming down his face, he could do no more than speak the first verse of the *De Profundis: Out of the depths have I cried unto Thee, O Lord!* . . . Shivering, he repeated the words: out of the depths! out of the depths!—and seemed to catch the muffled, despairing notes of his mother's voice far away in the country cemetery. . . . Polluted as he was, what could he do for his dead brother?

A cab took him on the first stage of his journey, then the train, in which he sat shut in with himself. Later, just as darkness was falling, in the city where he had been born, he took another train that would carry him on to the heaths and forests. He had to change once more, this time in a deserted station where he waited for two hours under the stars. The country of his earliest years came out to meet him. Dense walls of pine were already closing in on him, and in his nostrils was the familiar smell of marshy fields and turpentine. Not only in space had he left Fanny far behind: he had travelled back through time to the lost innocence of the dead years.

He was surprised to find how much younger his mother looked, as a result of living alone. She seemed thinner, gentler,

140

less shut away on the barren heights of authority. At first they talked of Joseph.

"The poor boy offered up to God each moment of his final agony," she said. "His faith was without blemish, and so, too, was his innocence. But which of us can stand without fear before the Judgment Seat? Which of us can be sure that he is justified in the eyes of the Almighty?"

Fabien recognized her old familiar tones—but it seemed now as though she were speaking the words from force of habit, merely. They were no longer in accord with a heart that was now like earth which has been softened by the rain.

When they got back from the cemetery he found a letter from Fanny. She had disguised her handwriting on account of Thérèse. The envelope felt heavy, and he dreaded to find within pages and pages filled with supplication. He walked down alone to the little stream. The frosty grass wet his shoes. He could hear the sucking sound of mud beneath his feet. From the letter came the smell that impregnated everything that Fanny touched. He was amazed that her scent should reach even into this country solitude, forcing its presence on the grassy void. The icy current, exposed now to the full light of day, flowed on beneath bare alders and between dead briars. A woodcock flew from a thicket, swift and heavy on the wing. The water had seeped into the holes made by rooting wild-boar. He heard the screaming of a sawmill, and it seemed to him as though the pine trunks were crying aloud in their agony. Without even opening the letter, he tore it into tiny scraps which soon the streamlet mingled with its frothy scum.

He went back to his mother and had, at once, a feeling that

she was about to wield the probe. She said that the curé would be celebrating Mass at seven o'clock.

"Tomorrow morning we shall be able to take Communion together in Joseph's memory. I have told the curé that you may wish to make your confession first."

She was arranging his inner life for him with that artless determination which she had shown when he was twelve years old. In his reply, he was moved less by anger than by the desire to start a quarrel (thereby making it possible to escape without rousing her suspicions).

"You forget how old I am, mother. It was no part of my intention to take Communion here."

She could not understand him, was voluble in protest. How could he not wish to do as she had suggested? He knew what value the intentions of the living have for the dead. . . . She could hardly believe that he would wish to deprive his brother of such aid. She spoke just as she had always done. It did not seem to occur to her that he might be different from the little pious boy he once had been, from the youth so strong in chastity. Suddenly worried, she turned her face to him, all drawn and tear-stained with the day's emotions. She was a million miles away from suspecting anything wrong in her son's conduct. What she dreaded much more was that his faith might be passing through a crisis. She had heard priests talking about new intellectual theories, about forms of heresy against which even the sacerdotal mind might not be wholly proof. Dryly, he cut her short.

"At least, my boy, set my mind at rest by telling me that your faith is unshaken?"

He begged her not to worry. She could be easy, he said, on

that score. If he possessed any certainty in the world it was the one that she had given him as a child. Now that he was grown up he had received ample confirmation of it.

She embraced him with a fervor that was unusual in her. But all that evening there was silence between them, and he, sitting with a book and pretending to read, could feel her eyes upon him. Nevertheless, they prayed together, and he felt as though he were no more than twelve and that his brother was close beside him, kneeling by the bed, his face buried in the counterpane. As of old, the words sounded muffled because Madame Dézaymeries kept her hands over her face. He found himself remembering a certain evening when, while his mother prayed, he had heard the sound made by Fanny as she turned the pages of a book, sitting by the fire, an exile from this act of family worship. He had, he recollected, twisted his head round and watched the young woman dangling a heelless velvet slipper from her toe. She had been stroking her cheek with an ivory paper knife, and smiled at the pious boy with a look of tender mockery.

He made no attempt to persuade his mother to join him in Paris. "It would be yielding to a weakness," she said . . . but she spoke in the tone of one whose dearest wish it is to yield. "It is just because," she went on, "I want it so much that I must give up the idea of such a trip." In the old days, when she had refused to take a proffered chance of happiness she had wasted no words on the matter. But now, in her softened, unfamiliar mood of loneliness, she added: "I don't seem, nowadays, to be able to live without you."

Fabien could think of nothing to say except "You must do what seems most sensible to you." The words were deceptive, but she would not let herself believe that they contained a hidden meaning. More than once she directed the conversation in such a way that he might return to the charge and spirit her off to Paris in spite of herself—but he said nothing. Until the very last evening she hoped that he would force her to go against her will, would take pity on her overpowering desire, would play an active hand in the sweet plot.

He left before dawn. His mother, with her hair down, and wearing a black dressing gown, stood by the kitchen range and watched him eat. "You're still here," she said, "but this evening you'll be in Paris," and she stroked his forehead and his cheeks as she never would have done when he was small. A farm hand came to carry down the bags. He had a lighted lantern, but put it out. The sky showed white in the puddles of the road. Factory sirens were calling men to work. The pines, with their branches spread wide like crosses, stood drowned in mist. The dawn sky looked as though it had been dragged down to meet their upward thrust and now engulfed their crests so that they were invisible to the resin-drawers busy at their work of enlarging the gashes in the trunks.

That evening, at the d'Orsay station, lost in the anonymous crowd lining the barrier, Fanny scrutinized the grubby faces of the travellers as they came up the stairs. Fabien always took his time. What message would she read in his eyes? His running away without seeing her again, his failure to answer her letter, had inclined her to expect the worst. The dead brother, she had felt, the gloomy heaths, the remorseless mother, would all have been in league against her. Then, that morning, a telegram had come telling her that he was on his way back, and she had begun to hope again. She felt the agonizing thrill of the gambler as she told herself that at any moment now she would know whether what lay before her was death—or life. Suddenly he appeared—the youngest member of all this dusty crowd, and, while he was still some distance from her, smiled. They did not even touch hands, but beneath his gaze she felt herself trembling with happiness. In the car it was he who first kissed her in the hollow of her neck. She said that she would go with him only as far as the door of his hotel. She must hurry back because of the girl.

"What girl?"

"Why, the girl I wrote about in the letter which you never answered. Donald brought her back with him from Brussels, where he's staying on for a few days. He'll be back this evening . . . you'll meet him. It'll all go off splendidly, you see if it doesn't."

He was afraid she might notice the wave of hot color that suddenly flooded his cheeks. He saw in imagination the torn scraps of the letter he had not read mingling with the scum of a moorland stream. He was prudent enough to let Fanny do the talking.

"I explained that it was Donald's darling daughter. I've found out since that he had a boy, too, by Leda Southers—think of it, he's ten years old! Naturally, he's his favorite. But he seems very proud of this Colombe of his. . . . What an idea, giving a girl a name like that—Colombe!"

"There was a parish of Sainte-Colombe quite close to where we used to live."

"Listen, darling. I've got to take the child to a concert this evening in the Champs-Élysées. Why not join us?"

He said that it wouldn't be quite the thing for him to go

to a public entertainment so soon after the anniversary of his brother's death. She burst out laughing. That must be another of Thérèse's ideas!

"My dear, only fools regard music as an entertainment. It's when I'm suffering most that I find I can't do without it. . . ."

She broke off, surprised that he did not protest, as he usually did whenever she brought Thérèse Dézaymeries into the conversation. Instead, he snuggled up against her like a little boy.

"You've no idea how *beastly* I was to mamma. . . . She was longing for me to bring her back. She just waited and waited for a word or a sign . . . and I was so frightened! It's horrible of me, because I do really love her. It's awful to think that now, when we've got such a short time in which we might be together, I can't bear the thought of having her with me. It's as though I were wishing she were dead. . . ."

"What big words! Don't be a little silly, my dear. All it means is that you're twenty and that you don't want your years of youth to be buried alive. . . ."

She followed him up the hotel's evil-smelling stairs. She loved, even more than the flat in the rue Visconti, this squalid room into which Fabien so seldom let her come. It was rich with the day-to-day animal smell of his presence. It was a constant joy to her to wash her hands with his used cake of soap, and dry them on the towel dirtied by his razor. Ever since the day when she had laid her cheek on the rough surface of his bolster and he had violently pulled her away, she loved to sit on the iron bedstead, the student's bedstead, the bedstead that, for her, was forbidden ground.

"Your youth does not wish to be buried alive. As somebody— I forget who—once said: Let the dead bury their dead."

"You're right, my sweet, it is better for the dead to stay with the dead. . . ."

The tone of his voice had changed. She dared not switch on the light, imagining the sudden look of desperation that had come to his face in the darkness.

"You know how fond I was of your poor mother. She drove me from the house, I know . . . but she's only got to hold out her arms. . . . All the same, darling, look at the existence she leads—her attitude of refusal to life."

"And how, may I ask, do you define life?"

"Life is love, my love. At least, that's the only thing I've ever expected of it, and I certainly have found it."

"More than once?"

Momentarily abashed, she took his hand:

"Often it was the shadow only. But even when you were little more than a child, I loved you. Once one has found the real thing, it doesn't matter, does it, how often one has been deceived? Your mother has never had anything. I wish you could know what her attitude to your father was—quite, quite too extraordinary! . . . Anyone looking at her now would take her for an old maid, don't you think so? I don't mean that as an insult, Fabien, but really no one would ever think that she had had children. That hard face of hers . . ."

She was afraid that he might turn on her in anger, but he gave no sign that he had taken her words in ill part. He merely said:

"You've never seen her face, have you, when she thinks no one is looking? There are days when she comes back after Mass, from the Calvary."

"What's the Calvary?"

"A hospital where she goes twice a week to look after the cancer patients. She looks positively radiant, then, I swear she does. . . . I think her face on those occasions is the only face in which I have ever seen real joy. . . ."

"When I am in your arms, Fabien, what do you see in *my* face?"

He replied that he had never dared to look at it.

"That, dear love, is because my joy is so terrible that it frightens you. I, too, know what joy means, *I* have had experience of it . . . of joy . . . of joy . . . of joy! . . ."

Her voice as she repeated the word grew harsh. Her face looked ugly because she was puckering up her eyes in an effort to keep back the tears. Fabien sat down on the bed and took her in his arms like a child. She lay sobbing against his shoulder.

As he was being driven to the theater, he thought: "Yes, let the dead bury their dead." He was surprised to find that he was feeling happy, perhaps because he had forced Fanny to confess her wretchedness, perhaps because at last he had made his choice, and had not consented to be numbered among the dead.

In Fanny's box there was one other woman. He ought to have known her but had to be freshly introduced. He never recognized women. He was fond of saying that every new dress is a disguise, and that there is no end to this playing of variations on the theme of clothes.

"And this is little Colombe, about whom I was speaking to you."

A young, decidedly tall girl rose awkwardly from her seat and held out a gloved hand (she had on the only pair of long gloves to be seen in the theater). Fabien thought her ugly but odd. His seat was behind hers. She must have scrubbed her neck with a rough towel, because the delicate skin showed red. Her hair had been dragged back so that it left, fully exposed, two tiny ears, the lobes of which looked flushed and swollen.

"They taught her to wear her hair like that at the convent," Fanny said to the strange woman. "Of course, it looks very ridiculous to us, but we should think it rather attractive if it happened to be the fashion, as it may well be, soon."

Fabien addressed himself to the girl: "Have you been living in a convent?"

Without looking at the young man, she said that she had been brought up by the Ladies of X . . . in Belgium—and then pretended to read her program, wrinkling her nose and letting a little frown of concentration appear between her rather Chinese-looking eyebrows, which Fabien decided were distinctly comic. Her voice, too, was comic. Suddenly she raised her face, threw a quick glance at Fabien, blushed a deep scarlet, and then looked down into the auditorium, where the orchestra was "tuning up." Finally she inquired whether the concert had begun. He replied, meaning to make her laugh, that with "this sort of music" one could never be sure. But she did not laugh. Instead, she examined the conductor with great care, after which she turned to Fabien and said with extreme seriousness: "No, they've not begun yet."

This childlike simplicity made him feel very happy. He found in it a satisfaction at once poignant and tender. He had the whole evening before him in which to look at her neck. It was long, and reminded him of a pouter pigeon—which exactly suited her name, for was she not called Colombe, Dove, Pigeon? Fanny had mentioned her in the letter which, at this very moment, must be eddying to and fro on the weedy surface of the stream. It pleased him to think that he had mingled the name and the image of this unknown child with the fresh flow of water which must now be shimmering beneath the moon, and, swaddled in mist, filling the darkness with its chaste murmurings.

"It's over!"

She had turned to him with an expression of infantile relief. She moved her arms and legs. A couple of sweets produced sudden bulges in her cheeks. She thought it wise of Fabien not to take any because "they stick to one's teeth so."

Fanny was staring through her opera glasses. "Look at Coco and the Princess down there in the stalls," she said to the strange lady. "They don't see us, but they can feel they're being looked at. We really must go down and say 'hullo.' . . . You won't mind, Fabien, will you?"

They pressed past him, plump and powdered. He breathed in their scent. He exchanged smiles with the young girl, wondered what he could find to say to her, and finally asked whether she was enjoying Paris.

"I'm frightened of people."

Her answer delighted him. He said he could see that she was still a *wild* pigeon, and that she ought really to have been called *Pal*ombe.

"It was mamma who wanted to call me Colombe, because in the town where she was born there was a parish where they used to have a procession in honor of Sainte-Colombe, and she played the part of the saint. I've seen a photograph of her holding a palm. . . ."

Fabien exclaimed that he too had been born in that same

town. Very soon they decided that they had probably met in the park, might even have played together.

"I was born in Paris," Colombe told him; "but mamma went back to B . . . because my guardian was director of the theater at that time and put her on the free list. Was it on Thursdays and Sundays that you went to the park, and what part of it, the duck pond or the terrace?"

"Oh, we used to run all over the place."

She gave him a long look and said that she was trying to remember whether she had ever known a dark-complexioned little boy.

"But I was much older than you, probably as much as five years older!"

"And then, of course, almost all the little boys in B . . . are dark-complexioned."

There had been only one fair boy in Fabien's form at school, and he had been nicknamed the "English kid."

"If that had been you I should have remembered."

He said in reply:

"My brother was really quite fair when he was a baby, but later on his hair turned chestnut. He was going to be a priest, but he died."

"Oh, I'm so terribly sorry, because it always makes me unhappy, not having any brothers or sisters, and I used to think how nice it would be if mamma would ask God whether she couldn't have some more children. But to have had a brother and then to have lost him! He must have been sweet and gentle to want to be a priest. Perhaps you teased him, because I expect you weren't always good-natured. . . . Oh, they're going to start again."

The Weakling and the Enemy

Fanny and her friend came back into the box. Fabien shut his eyes. What did it matter to him what they were playing? He imposed the rhythm of his own heart on the din made by the orchestra. Not for anything in the world would he have kept his eyes on his mistress' really lovely back. He infinitely preferred the fresh, frail reed before him, the mists of childhood just dispersing, the angular shoulders of his budding Eve.

"I can't find the sleeve," laughed Fanny as Fabien helped her, rather awkwardly, into her evening coat. Someone took it from him with an air of authority. Looking round he saw Donald Larsen.

"I think we've met before, haven't we, Monsieur Dézaymeries? At Venice, if I'm not wrong?"

They exchanged a few more words and shook hands. The giant himself wrapped the young girl up very carefully, and with a strange show of haste propelled her toward the exit. Fanny whispered to Fabien:

"Tomorrow, at our house. . . . Didn't you notice how polite he was to you?"

He made no reply. His whole mind was concentrated for the moment on how to get himself into a position where the girl would see him. She had already moved some distance away, but turned her head to look for him. At last she picked him out and smiled a good-night.

He felt wildly happy striding through the darkness—though what had caused his happiness he did not know. There was nothing to warn him that it was as though an angel had passed through his life, an angel who would not return. It did not occur to him that his mood was due to his meeting this young girl, because he had been conscious of it before he had even seen her, when the train, that morning, had carried him away from the burned-up land of melancholy, away from his mother. It had reached its apogee after his talk with Fanny when she had cried and talked of joy.

He followed the pavement that runs beside the Seine. The river lay swathed in mist. Just so, at this very moment, must the stream look in that remote countryside of his. A wreathing smoke was rising from the water as it must have done in the days when the present stone embankments were a wilderness of trees and rushes. It smelled of the days before history had begun.

Suddenly, with his elbows pressed to his side, and his bare head thrown back, the young man broke into a long, loping run. He did not stop until he had reached the Alexander Bridge. There he crossed to the further bank, with no more idea of where he was going than a homing pigeon. If only there was someone he could talk to! He did not know a soul. Could it be that he had not a single friend? By this time he had started down the Boulevard Raspail. Shortly after passing the Croix-Rouge he recognized the house where Jacques Maïnz lived, a colleague of his at the École des Chartes, with whom his work had sometimes brought him in contact. Maïnz was the best man of his year. He was a Jew, and on one occasion had said to Fabien: "You've the luck to be a believing Catholic, and yet you don't become a Benedictine. I can't think why not." The young man smiled at the recollection. He saw that his friend was burning the midnight oil, and, without stopping to think, called Maïnz's name to the concierge, and, though it was nearer to one o'clock than to midnight, knocked at his fellow-student's door.

A voice asked suspiciously who was there.

153

The Weakling and the Enemy

"It's me, Dézaymeries."

"My dear chap! at this time of night? What's the matter?"

Sobered by this welcome, Fabien looked at his host. The man might have been any age. Weak eyes peered out from behind a pair of circular spectacles. Suddenly it struck him what a gulf separated his own burning heart from this other heart of ice. He excused his presence by saying that he wanted to copy out some notes of a lecture which he had missed.

"Yes, I know. You *are* getting a bit slack, Dézaymeries, and you could pass so high if only you'd do a little work. Why, I used to look on you as a rival."

Jacques Maïnz gazed at the tall, bareheaded young man whose open overcoat revealed his evening dress. Fabien had followed him into his workroom.

"Here you are, but I must have that notebook back the day after tomorrow without fail. . . . Just a moment, I'll show you where the automatic switch is."

On the landing he added, in a tone in which contempt, affection and envy were strangely mixed:

"You're far too good-looking, you know, to make a scholar."

These farewell words served to rekindle the young man's flickering flame of happiness. He was walking slowly now, weighed down by a load of delicious heaviness. So people thought him handsome, did they? and little Colombe had liked looking at him this evening! He thought of her, at first confusedly, then with a visual precision that embarrassed him—of her shoulder, of the narrow expanse of arm where her long glove ended. . . . He closed his eyes and shook his head in the comical way he had had as a child when he wanted to get rid of a "wicked" thought. But why, now that he had tasted of the

154

fruit of the tree, should he fight against his sense of gushing happiness? He remembered how once, when he was with Fanny at a circus, he had seen a sudden jet of dirty water squirted over the tan, lifting odds and ends of straw and dust, and making a muddy lake, the level of which slowly rose. He wanted to save little Colombe from his own unclean and detailed thoughts—but could not resist the temptation to dirty her with that knowingness which he had learned from another.

In his shabby room he went to bed without a light.

9

FANNY was delighted, next day, to find that he was more ardent, more restlessly expectant, than she ever remembered having seen him. What she did not know was that his mood of desire was linked with the feeling of disgust that always oppressed him, but had now been carried to such an unusual degree of intensity that it resulted in a hatred of which he was ashamed and fearful, because he could not understand the reason for it. When he thanked her because none of the furniture had been moved during his absence, she told him not to infer that her business was doing badly. All it meant was that she had gone into partnership with the Comte de X . . . and thought it better to house her stuff with him. In that way prospective customers would think that the bits and pieces were old family heirlooms, and would be prepared to pay a high price for their mistake. . . . She laughed so loudly that she did not see his sudden flush, his expression of loathing, the furtive look which he turned toward the door. While she was tidying her hair in front of a triple mirror she was able to study him without turning her head. All she realized was that she had torn the old wound open again. She tried to soft-pedal what she had just said, explaining that she had merely wanted him to "see things as they were." But the wound was open and bleeding. She was afraid that he might refuse to dine at her house that evening; but he agreed to do so with a gay alacrity which brought her some degree of reassurance.

Had he not been seated some distance away on her left, Fanny would have realized to what it was she owed his seeming impatience and happiness. He paid no attention to the other guests (English people whose language he did not understand). He spent his whole time staring at the young girl who sat at the far end of the table, her head leaning slightly to one side, her bare arms looking decidedly cold. Her hair, dressed in the Chinese fashion which left her rather bulbous forehead uncovered, gave her the air of belonging to another period. She was wearing round her neck a child's necklace adorned with sacred medals, and each time she caught his eye she replied, as best she could, with a narrowing of the lids, a melancholy smile, a pout of her rather full lips—all intended to express her annoyance at being so far away, but also, though she did not know it, conveying the impression of a kiss. So long as she was there Fabien felt no need to close his eyes or shake his head in an effort to drive away evil thoughts. He could see in the young body, lit, as it were, from within, all the signs of a sensitive conscience, of uncertainty and confused scruples—of some imperfectly understood mood of renunciation. But before their glances could meet they had to cross a danger zone. Donald Larsen, seated opposite Fanny, may have had a suspicion of their unspoken colloquy. He was eating greedily, drinking more greedily still, and talking hardly at all. His complexion passed through all the stages from pink to brick-red, and, finally, to purple. Several times Fabien was conscious that the china-blue eyes were fixed on him as they had been in Venice.

The Weakling and the Enemy

As soon as the ice had been served, Donald made a sign to the girl, and she disappeared. Fanny said with a laugh, "The sandman's coming." Fabien remembered how she used to say that each evening at nine o'clock in Madame Dézaymeries' room, and how she had drawn him to her for a good-night kiss.

He did not see his wild pigeon again that evening, but was happy in the thought that she must be feeling sad.

He took the same way home as on the previous night, but his mood was melancholy and he walked more slowly. No longer did he leap like a chamois in the mist. It was his first evening of tender reverie. He felt absolutely safe, knowing that among all these ravaged hearts his was the only one on which his wild pigeon would choose to alight, because corruption, in his case, had not progressed beyond the initial stage. Only twenty-two years had elapsed since his coming into the world. Who can corrupt the spring? Where his mother had made a mistake was in not realizing that the body, too, can be sanctified. A young man and a young girl blaze in the face of God like two high, clear flames. Drawn into one another, they show the brighter. He understood many things of which his mother was ignorant. He found a glory in realizing that he had no need to protect his love from his muddied thoughts of yesterday. He revelled in that knowledge, quite forgetting that, thanks to physical ecstasies still recent, the demon in him was temporarily sated.

Two nights later, seated at the same table between a couple of Englishmen, it was he who sought a pretext for silence. In the first place, he had been in an agony of apprehension because his wild pigeon had not been in the drawing room. But she slipped into the dining-room with the guests, and, since there were no other women present, Donald made her sit on his right. She smiled at Fabien, but as though through prison bars. The whole situation should have warned him that somebody was doing his best to keep them apart. But if he had any suspicions they were directed solely at Fanny. He felt reassured when he saw that she was deeply involved with her English neighbor in one of those doubtless æsthetic discussions which she pursued so enthusiastically that at moments she seemed almost to be losing her temper. Fabien told himself that he would not look at the girl before the second course. But, though he did not see his wild pigeon, he could hear her fluttering in her invisible cage. She was worried by his feigned indifference. Unable any longer to keep the promise he had made to himself, he directed at her a long and ardent gaze, and saw the little face with its prominent forehead redden with a mixture of love and shame. At the same moment he was aware that Donald Larsen was staring at him in a quite intolerable manner. He pretended to be occupied with a piece of mural decoration, but the china-blue eyes were insistent. As in Venice, this man, without uttering a single word, had voiced an entreaty with a look, so, this evening, he managed to convey by the same means a clear-cut prohibition, an obvious threat. Fabien, who had just drunk a glass of Johannisberger, felt annoyed because of the sense of embarrassment and fear that was oppressing him. He made up his mind to defy the man with the pink cheeks, whose manners, so he told himself, were those of a drunkard. It was a matter of general knowledge that, from five o'clock on, Donald Larsen was never fully under control, though he was skilful at disguising the fact. It was an understood thing that no one should ever talk to him at meals, but this evening, the young Englishman on Fabien's right, was making a polite effort to say something to him in French. He was explaining that he was an army officer, and that none of his comrades ever suspected him of writing poetry or of contributing to magazines. He never talked literature in the mess: to have done so would have more or less disgraced him. Only once had he been able to refer to a poem, because it happened to deal with fox-hunting. Fabien slowly raised his eyes and steeled himself briefly to endure the stare of the giant who, for the last ten minutes, had been drinking nothing. Then he sought the eyes of the girl, who was leaning forward in his direction, feeling his attraction as a sunflower might the sun.

It was only because Fanny's argument had become strident and because everyone else at the table was joining in that nobody noticed the terrible expression in Donald Larsen's face—the white, expressionless stare, the trembling upper lip, the glass shaking in his fingers. "He can't do anything to you," said Fabien to himself; "it doesn't matter to you what *he* wants. What is he, anyhow, if it comes to that?" No one in Paris was more looked down upon. Besides, hadn't he trafficked in his own wife? But what the young country-bred man most strongly felt was the peasant's distrust and hatred of the man of uncertain origins, of the nomad, the mountebank. "No one knows where this Larsen comes from: a Dane fathered by a German Jew!" Fabien out-stared the loathsome jailer with a feeling of delight. Slowly the girl turned her head away. One hand was raised to her rather exposed throat. What would the giant do? The veins were standing out on his temples, and fury was making him sway like a beech-tree. Fabien expected an outburst. If only he too could give his anger rein! He would not mince words! If necessary, he would go for this Goliath physically. But suddenly Goliath grew calm. He leaned toward Colombe and his purple lips began to move close to her flushed little ear. At his first words she stared stupidly at Fabien, then, seemingly, voiced a protest. But the man interrupted her, and she listened in silence. "Look at the old man making up to his daughter!" Colombe directed a quick, terrified glance at Fabien while the purple lips went on muttering. With the whole table between them, what could Fabien do to counter the deadly things the swine was saying? She asked Larsen a question, to which he replied with a melancholy seriousness. Fabien saw her suddenly flush scarlet. He knew that the blow had come!—could feel it strike home in his own flesh. He had no idea what, precisely, had been the blow the man had aimed, but he felt as though he had received a mortal wound. His neighbor asked him whether he was feeling unwell. Fabien gave him a terrified stare, but said nothing. He saw Donald Larsen pass his napkin over his face, which had suddenly become convulsed by a fit of coughing which set his scarlet jowl quivering. Of what nature was the secret with which he had overpowered the innocent girl? Her narrow, childish face had hardened. She was crushing a rosebud in her hand and picking off its petals one by one. Fabien wanted to cry aloud: "Whatever he has been saying about me, don't believe it!"—but he had to sit there motionless, correct, a silent witness of his own death. If only he could have caught her eye!—but she seemed no longer to be aware of his presence. He had ceased to exist for her; he had just been murdered. At last Fanny got up. Another minute and Fabien would no longer have been able to contain himself. In the drawing room the girl handed round the coffee. He waited for the moment when she would approach him.

The Weakling and the Enemy

But, having served all the other guests, she gave him a look of contempt which left him in no doubt of her deliberate avoidance, and passed on. He followed her into the passage, heard a door shut and the sound of a key turning in the lock.

He made for his usual refuge, a small empty drawing room, now completely deserted. It was filled with lacquer furniture, and a single lamp gave light to its equivocal intimacy. Stretched on a divan, he began to smoke Turkish cigarettes, lighting them one after the other, endlessly. On a low table, within reach of his hand, glittered a decanter of sweet wine. Several times he filled and emptied a long-stemmed glass, striving to attain to a state of besotted insensibility, sleep, a death that should be eternal. If only he could get rid of the obsessive thought that Donald Larsen had not even had to lie about him! "In order to pass sentence of death upon me in the girl's eyes, he had only to explain the meaning of my presence in this house. . . . I expect he implied that I was a kept man. I'm twenty-two, and Fanny is almost an old woman. . . . Would it do any good to write to her? I bet he keeps a careful eye on the letters she gets. . . . What bliss it would be never to see Fanny again . . . and if she dies of it, well, let her. . . . No, no, I mustn't say that. Besides, if I were separated from Fanny it would mean that I should be separated from the girl as well. . . . Nothing to do but drink. . . . " He longed to sleep, and when, finally, sleep overcame him, lay with his head thrown back against the cushions. His arm slipped limply from the divan. His hand lay like a dead thing on the carpet.

He had a confused feeling that someone else was in the room, but did not immediately open his eyes. He could hear the sound of breathing. A young man was standing by him. Where had he seen him already? The frail torso above the over-developed thighs looked as though it had been poured into the short jacket. The clean-shaven face showed blue round the thick lips. Fabien recognized the voice as Cyrus Bargues'.

"Did I wake you up?—how *beastly* of me! There's something so *mysterious,* don't you think, when people are asleep—*young* people, I mean, of course. To see an *old* man asleep is like watching a dress-rehearsal of the stroke that's going to carry him off! *Actually,* my dear, I don't expect you to thank me. . . . All the same . . . in Venice. . . ."

He broke off because Fabien, his hair tousled, his fists clenched and a glowering expression on his face, looked as though he might be about to attack him. But the mingled fumes of sweet wine and Turkish cigarettes made him fall back again on the cushions. He was already half drunk, and there was no longer room in his mind for anything so clear-cut as hatred, disgust or distress. As though he were imparting some profound secret, he said:

"There are, you know, such things as legitimate caresses."

Cyrus broke into a guffaw of strident laughter. He declared that he knew of no caresses that were not legitimate. Fabien replied in tones of the deepest gravity:

"There are such things: of that there can be no doubt—no doubt at all. But we men are so naturally responsive to caresses that they give us a wonderful illusion of infinity—and therein lies danger."

"Therein lies their charm, is what you mean, my dear. You really are the most *delicious* of creatures, quite *entrancing* . . . but to be avoided when you're sober. What you need is another drink. We'd better go by the passage and down the back stairs, so as to avoid our hosts."

At a bar in the rue Duphot they started in on whisky. Fabien achieved a mood of exaltation which brought him relief and peace of mind. Everything was turning out exactly as he wanted it to. He would discard Fanny like a bundle of old rags. Either she would kill herself or she wouldn't. The choice was hers! The only thing he cared about was to get back to his wild pigeon. It needed only a word from him and she would understand and forgive. They would go away somewhere and live far from the haunts of men with the pine trees of his childhood for company. . . . Who was this young man whispering in his ear and pressing him to drink? Seemed a good sort—was saying the dance must be purged of all ornament, made hieratic and expressive of ecstasy. But why should Cyrus want to leave this warm, cosy bar where women sat perched on stools looking like ibises? (he had never seen an ibis). . . . In the cloakroom they all used the same lipstick. . . . Cyrus led him outside. The street was as moist and as warm as a mouth. In the next bar, in spite of the frantic din made by the band, Fabien no longer felt happy. He took a cocktail and it made him sad. With the second his feeling of joy became slowly immersed in a dark flood. He kept on repeating like an imbecile, "Colombe—Sainte-Colombe—little Sainte-Colombe." Cyrus said that, personally, he found her too old for a little girl and too young for a woman.

"You have turned up either too soon or too late. Besides, make no mistake about it, the old man's got ambitions for that child of his. He has suddenly noticed that there beats within

164

his breast a father's heart. He is aiming to find a husband for her from the very tip-top drawer—some superannuated peer or glittering maharajah—they *are* to be found, you know, if only one looks in the right places. . . . Hullo, now you're crying! You look so *funny,* my dear, just like a small boy!"

No woman, he went on, had ever made *him* cry. He loved nothing but his art. Women always needed so much reassuring. One had got to be forever stroking and petting them like animals.

By this time Fabien was quite incapable of controlling his movements. In an effort to blow his nose he upset both their glasses, after which he sank into a doze. When he emerged from it, Cyrus was saying that he had tried cocaine once, when he had been going through hell because of somebody whose name he wouldn't mention.

"But it doesn't soothe one as much as they say it does. The only effect it had on me was to make me *terribly* irritable. A curtain in my room had only to be crooked. . . . It was dancing that saved me."

Somewhat later he said:

"Don't cry, you little silly. The only thing in life that matters is to be twenty-two. . . . A time will come when one will no longer be an object of desire to anyone. There is only one form of perfect happiness—to know that one is surrounded by a thousand fierce desires, to hear about one the crackling of branches. . . . "

Fanny was tolerant of Fabien's escapade; was even pleased to think that he had gone on the loose. She had her own ingenious methods of getting rid of the effects of his night out. Long experience had taught her how to deal with the morning after. But she did say: "What on earth have you done to Donald to make him so mad at you? The moment I try to put in a good word for you he jumps down my throat. You've no idea what coarse language he uses in front of the child, too. It won't be long before the bloom's rubbed off *her*! Why are you making such a face? Are you in pain, my pet?"

She thoroughly enjoyed arranging his pillows, laying cool hands on his forehead, behaving like a young mother comforting her big son. With his haggard cheeks and mournful expression he looked so like the little Fabien whom once she had taken on her knees! She even ventured to mention Thérèse Dézaymeries, and grew slightly sentimental. The only gentleness she had known in her life, she said, was associated in her mind with evenings spent in Thérèse's room. Did Fabien remember the gray wallpaper and the enlarged Nadar photograph of his father? The lamp had had a shade of pink ribbed glass, and they had loved running their fingers up and down the grooves when they were small boys.

"You used to sit on a stool at our feet, and, when you looked at me, your eyes were full of innocence, uncertainty and dreams. You played silent games in the dark corner between your little white bed and your mother's *prie-Dieu*."

Fanny was remembering the whisper of the rain, the crackling of the fire and the boy's low muttering. She had come to that room from very far away, dropping to rest in the quiet lamp-light like a tired bird. She had made one with those innocent hearts and simple things. One evening, Fabien, his face pressed to the crossbars of the window, had been playing a game which consisted in trying to follow the movements of one single swallow among all the bewildering dartings of its fellows. She had thought that he looked like the imprisoned Dauphin. She could never, afterwards, hear the cries of swifts on country roofs without seeing again, in imagination, the stuffy room, and Thérèse, all anxiety lest she miss the devotions of the Month of Mary in the Cathedral. . . .

She stopped talking, realizing that he was asleep. Never before had she been so deeply impressed by the look of chastity on his virile face, by that nobility which marks the faces of young men whom it is a woman's mission to corrupt, but which no soiling can destroy: the last trace of childhood, hovering like a patch of mist impervious to the midday sun. She touched the smooth forehead with her lips as she had seen his mother do, straightened his blankets, and was still at her post when night fell, lost in dreams beside the sleeping youth.

10

FANNY had asked the young man not to come again to the Quai Debilly until after Donald Larsen had left on his next trip to London.

"I just don't know what's biting him. Are you sure you've said nothing to annoy him? And the child's playing up to him! He's putting her against me, against both of us. What on earth can he be up to? I just pretend not to understand all his vulgar hints and innuendos. . . . Darling, *don't* look so tragic! Donald Larsen's scarcely in a position to spread scandal about anyone. I wouldn't say it except to you, but mark my words, it's a good deal more dangerous to have him as a friend than as an enemy. . . . The only thing that matters is that he shan't separate *us*. After all, he's utterly dependent on me, and he knows perfectly well that my whole life is wrapped up in you."

With her head on Fabien's shoulders she begged him in vain to show her a little affection. It was a dark afternoon in the gloomy depth of winter. Fortunately, the low lamp shone only on the young man's hands and knees. His face, with its expression of hatred and repulsion, was invisible. . . . Until Donald Larsen's next trip to London . . . could he hold out so long? He brought himself, nowadays, to endure Fanny's presence only because he knew that if he gave her up he would lose all hope of winning his wild pigeon. But now that he could not see the girl, he found it agony to play the lover with a woman whom he detested. But his performance, alas! was too bad to deceive his former mistress, though she still believed that it was because of his religious scruples that he had turned from her. She never dreamed of looking for any other reason to explain his bitterness and lack of ardor. But it was not God who stood between her and Fabien. The wretched youth had certainly not ceased to believe in what once had been the whole of life for him, but he *had* accepted the fact that he was now dead to that life. He had consented to leave the ship, had landed on a coast of dust and ashes. There was no hope that the vessel would ever return to rescue his wrecked soul. He was prepared to envisage what once would have filled him with horror. If it was Fanny's destiny to kill herself, then kill herself she must. He could no longer bring himself to put his arms protectingly about that worn and used-up body. Often, in the course of the sunless winter, sitting on the iron bedstead in his hotel room with its low ceiling and its mingled smell of soap and tobacco, when he ought to have been at his class, or working in one of the libraries, he surrendered himself to the desire of a sleep from which there should be no awakening. The idea fascinated him. But he had no belief in the possibility of such a sleep, and he was afraid of God.

Since the night he had spent with the dancer making the rounds of the bars, though he had not again got drunk, he had taken to drinking rather more at his meals than good sense allowed, and just enough to produce a temporary feeling of exaltation. At such moments he imagined himself sitting outside a café looking on to an unfamiliar landscape, with Colombe at his side gazing at him. He felt like a man armed and vigorous, vigorous enough to fight his way to her through all difficulties, to calm her fears, to overcome her resistance. . . . But later, back once more in his low-ceilinged room, poisoning himself with tobacco, he would wander from bed to window, from window to bed, a prey to uncertainty. "If I did carry you off, my poor little pigeon, what should I do with you? Would my mother welcome a girl born out of wedlock, and with such a father? And could *I* ever feel love for a son of mine who had in his veins the blood of a Larsen? My own children would be objects of horror to me."

It was on these lines that his thoughts were running when Fanny took his face in her two hands, bent above his eyes with their absent look, and said:

"What are you thinking about?"

He replied ill-temperedly: "Not about you."

He broke from her. Wearily, Fanny tied her veil, not even bothering to look at herself in the glass. She was now in a mood of violent self-pity.

"You won't have much longer to wait: you'll be rid of me a good deal sooner than you think. But won't you just give me *one* look? You haven't looked at me since I came in. When I'm in your arms I seek in vain to read your baffled eyes. It is as though something in you were running away from me, were trying to put an infinite distance between us. But take care! . . ."

"Isn't what I leave behind enough to satisfy you?"

"Your body, you mean? . . . The body is everything and nothing. It is of value only because of *that*—I don't know what—that something which you take from it before you hand it over. . . . *You're* the one who gives yourself like a . . ."

The Weakling and the Enemy

The word was crude. He opened the door and, without looking at her, said:

"Get out! Get out!"

She stopped for a moment on the threshold. "It will have been your doing, Fabien." A moment later she was in the street. For all his earlier mood, the threat had its effect upon him. He hurried after her and caught her up at the corner of the rue Bonaparte. She was walking fast, like a woman pursued. Some of the people she passed turned to look at her. When she reached the river she had to slow down. They were side by side now, moving through the mist. A young street urchin followed them with his eyes: perhaps they had roused a sense of envy in him. Fabien said that he was suffering, and that when he was suffering he was an impossible companion. She thought that he was alluding to what she called his mystical day-dreaming. Would he never rid himself of all that nonsense? How dared *he* talk of suffering—a young man of twenty-two who had someone to love him? Had he any idea what she, after this unspeakable afternoon, was going to find when she got home? A girl to whom she was devoted, but who was now turned against her, a girl whose air of contempt was utterly exasperating; a man who put up with her merely because he found her necessary. No good mincing words: at bottom Donald detested her, but he knew that on her depended the bulk of his fortune. If she hadn't a positive genius for picking up old furniture, if she hadn't learned all about the picture racket, what would become of Larsen with all his grandiose but ruinous schemes?

She was at the end of her tether and stopped dead. They hailed a taxi. She continued with the tale of her woes.

The Weakling and the Enemy

"Never any let-up for me! This evening I've got to go to the Cirque Médrano with the pair of them, because Donald, who's got some supper engagement or other, insists on my being there to take the child home. Can't you imagine what fun that drive back will be for me in the company of a self-righteous and hostile little miss!"

Fabien asked her why she didn't leave Larsen. She replied that she no longer felt strong enough or brave enough to live alone.

"And who would have me now, Fabien?"

He turned away without replying. Having dropped her at her door, he went home on foot. He, too, would go to the circus that evening. The thought helped him to bear the burden of existence. He must learn how to get what enjoyment he could out of small, brief pleasures. Walking in Paris was, he had found, the best way of escaping from his troubles. Sometimes he would wake from his fits of dreaming in the middle of the road with traffic swirling round him. Tonight he reached his room without having the slightest idea of the route he had taken. He was surprised to see a light shining from under his door. Jacques Maïnz, his fellow-student at the École des Chartes, had been waiting for three-quarters of an hour. This was the first time he had ever paid Fabien a visit. He apologized for intruding on his privacy in this way, but the matter about which he had come was urgent. The Director was thinking of taking disciplinary measures against Dézaymeries on the ground that he absented himself from half his lectures.

"Don't you know any doctor who would give you a bogus certificate? That'd do the trick. There's a friend of mine; I'd gladly give you an introduction."

The Weakling and the Enemy

Fabien looked at the mass of untidy hair, at the pimply face, at the eyes which would have been fine if they had not grown dim from poring over manuscripts. The whole man was a product of laborious days spent in a library. He said:

"Don't worry your head about me. I'm sending in my resignation tomorrow."

Until this moment such an idea had never even entered his head, but he knew now, beyond all possibility of doubt, that his decision was irrevocable. It had been maturing in his mind without his being aware of it.

"D'you mean to say that you're leaving, Dézaymeries?"

"Why should you care?"

Maïnz, without moving from his chair, raised his lashless eyes and looked at Fabien.

"I shall miss you. True, we've never been friends, and I never really believed we could be. All the same, I liked to see you enjoying life. You brought—how shall I put it?—romance and color into the place. . . . Don't shrug your shoulders and look sullen. As a matter of fact, I think you're perfectly right to clear out. You never really belonged to us. I had a pretty good idea of the way your mind was working. . . . I suppose it surprises you to hear a 'dirty Jew' talking like this?"

"I've never confided in you."

"Yes you have, often, though you didn't know it. For instance, one day when we were talking about Saint Catherine of Siena you trotted out a whole theory of the nature of love. You described the frantic appetite that can never be strangled, the appetite that only we ourselves can divert God-wards. You told me that no human being can remain stationary, that the Infinite is a river and that we've got to go either upstream or down—up

173

to God our source, or down to the desperation of a nameless bitterness. There is, you said, such a thing as a sort of reversed perfection, the possibility of becoming always more and more criminal. . . . You see, you can't get away from your Catholic heritage. And all the time you were talking—we were leaning together over the same facsimile—I was conscious of a sort of fragrance. You're not the kind of chap who uses scent. . . . Now don't get mad. You see, I admire and envy you. Had I been of your faith, I should have been precisely the same sort of person I am now, doing exactly the same work, the only difference being that I should be wearing a monk's habit and living in some abbey or other. But in a chap like you the Catholic religion produces a whole crop of conflicts and private dramas. . . ."

The man was wholly devoid of tact. There was a heavy quality about his laughter. But Fabien, as a rule so quick to take offense, hung his head. It was with an air of humility that he replied:

"There's something I want to beg of you, Maïnz, and that is that you won't judge the tree by its rotten fruit—which is what I am . . . promise me."

"It seems to me very curious and interesting, Dézaymeries, that you should say a thing like that, that you should be obsessed by a scruple of that kind. The rest of us will just turn into archivists. Like everyone else in the world, we have found our particular mill, and we shall spend our lives turning it (in my case, it might just as well have been a lawyer's practice, an office or a factory). Rimbaud was perfectly right when he said, '*La main à plume vaut la main à charrue. Quel siècle à mains.*' Fundamentally, all a man cares about is stupefying himself. Intensity of life can be found equally well in business or drink.

The Weakling and the Enemy

Work, too, is a narcotic, and action, after all, is a form of sleep. Well, you have chosen life. Who was it said that the inner life is the only reality? My dear fellow, there are only two types of person that I admire: those, like you, who, instead of dissipating their energies in action, are self-creators, achieving self-mastery and enduring self-loss only to find themselves again triumphantly in an emotional struggle for a stake which is God—and those wise men of the East who also find their way to the divine, but by a different and perhaps a surer route; those for whom sanctity is detachment, who say of themselves that they have been 'delivered from the prison of life.' . . . Forgive me if I say that I think they have chosen the better part. I have a feeling that Buddha was, on the whole, the supreme example of human greatness. . . ."

"That's because you have no knowledge of Christ."

Maïnz, who was striding up and down the room, which was so small that the smoke from their two cigarettes shrouded the whole of its contents in mist, stopped in front of the tall, bitter young man whose tormented expression he guessed rather than saw.

"I know something of him, Dézaymeries, because I know you. . . ."

Fabien shook his head:

"He is in me no longer," he said, and repeated the words— "He is in me no longer."

"My poor young Christian, how wrong you are. Why, he possesses you entirely, rends you in twain, tears you from every foothold, detaches you from life at every moment of every day. . . ."

"I say again—don't judge the tree by its rotten fruit. There *are* Christians who can be joyful."

"I know that, my friend. I have made notes on the joys of Christians according to Pascal (you remember his letter to Mademoiselle de Roannez?). I have read the wildly joyful Odes of your poet Claudel."

In a low voice, Fabien said: "I am in torment!"

It was the first time in his life that he had ever confided in a friend, and the experience brought him a secret sweetness. This evening he had met the Jew who was called Simon of Cyrene.

He forgot all about dinner and turned up punctually at the circus. The place smelled of tan and clean stables. He remembered the Thursday long ago when he had gone with Joseph to the circus at Bordeaux. It was the one and only time that their mother had consented to take them. What mingled feelings of wonder and terror he had known on that occasion! . . . They had left before the end because there was to be a ballet. The fag-end of daylight had been hanging about the Place des Quin-conces. The fair was emptying. The damp evening breeze was rapidly dissipating the smell of hot coffee and waffles. He had a headache as the result of laughing so much. He felt detached from all the trivial daily round. His mother said they must hurry. There would be only just time to get their homework finished before dinner.

With a trembling hand he snatched up his opera glasses. The "wild pigeon" was sitting in the front of a box. Fanny looked gross and heavy. She was wearing a frock cut too low in the neck for such an occasion. Larsen's shirt-front glinted. Suddenly Fabien noticed that his wild pigeon had changed. She had lit a cigarette, and looked comic because she smoked it as though she were sucking a stick of barley sugar. She laughed with a great deal of grimacing, and turned to Larsen. She was probably saying that she felt "positively *drunk*" and that she was "laughing herself *sick.*" What innocence could stand out for long against the poisonous atmosphere diffused by Fanny? Evil is as infectious as any disease.

Somewhat later he saw her reddening her lips. She was laughing loudly, and a young man in a neighboring box leaned forward to look at her. Fabien told himself that if he could bring himself to renew his visits to the Quai Debilly there might still be time to save her from sinking altogether into the mire.

There was no need for him to pull his hat down over his eyes. These thousands of laughing faces were concentrated on the antics of the Fratellini Brothers. Colombe would never notice him in this dark, surging crowd which rippled with mirth like water under a stiff breeze. There was still time to rescue her. Might he not, by doing so, find his own way back to a state of grace? What else was there for him to do with his life? Fanny, in any case, was lost utterly. No man can save a corpse. He would sacrifice her in the cause of his wild pigeon. . . . Larsen, by failing to acknowledge his paternity, had no legal hold over her. Madame Dézaymeries would give her consent provided he could persuade her that his marriage was a duty, an obligation and not a pleasure. They would live the whole year round in the country—*his* country. . . .

There was a sudden blare of music, and the laughter of the audience was drowned by the din of the brass. A number of trick riders were dashing round the ring lightly poised on the shining cruppers of their horses. . . .

What sort of life would they lead in that remote countryside? He trembled with anticipated pleasure, thinking of the nights they would spend together in the sparsely furnished room smelling of pitch pine. In imagination he could hear the cocks crowing from farm to farm, and the hooting of owls, sounds that would make a background to young love with nothing in it of sin. Unconsciously, his mind took the direction of what Maïnz had said. The thought of an existence that should be all a conquest of the spirit, a process of interior mastery, enchanted him. Deep in the happiness of his home he would again find God. . . . The passages would echo to the noise of children's feet. . . . The lamp would shine upon their faces as they sat nodding sleepily over books. He would saunter with his pigeon through the dark garden. She would say: "I can't see the path." . . . Light would show red in the windows, or perhaps cut hearts of fire in the shutters.

He felt hungry and decided to leave during the interval. It is easier to think when one is walking. How many plans for a life in the country are brought to a head in the streets of Paris! . . . One last look at Colombe in her box and he was off, striding through the night, a tireless child of the heathlands, striving, without success, to deaden with physical fatigue the clamors of his lusty blood. Solitude! solitude! He would have liked to take up his conversation with Maïnz where it had been left. And then, suddenly, he began to think again of Fanny. Could one go on living if there was always with one the memory of a woman whom one had driven to her death? But perhaps she would *not* kill herself. "The main thing is not to go on committing adultery. That's where my strict duty lies." Any priest would tell him that. Besides, there was always the fact of grace, the reality of prayer, to be taken into account. Fanny would *not* be abandoned. He bit his lower lip and murmured to himself: "Hypocrite! filthy hypocrite!" . . . He had something cold to eat at Weber's, and drank champagne. Alone at his table he felt cut off from the rest of mankind. All of a sudden he was swept by a gust of happiness. Would he have liked to have Colombe there beside him at the moment? No. . . . Suppose she had gone from him forever, suppose she were dead, suppose he were handed a letter which she had written and addressed to him before she died? He composed its contents in imagination, and the tears welled into his eyes so that he had to hide his face. Oh, yes, he loved her, of that there could be no doubt at all; he loved her. But, in that future time, when they should be married and living remotely in the country, the thought of love would not be always, as it was with Fanny, in the forefront of their minds, a sickening obsession, an idiotic futility. Life, real life, has something better to bother about. The first thing for him to do was to get some order into the chaos of his thoughts. Now that the appalling hurricane had roared through him and passed on, he must settle down and write, live for the service of truth, be at once famous and alone, inaccessible to the crowd, yet known to all the world.

11

NEXT day Fabien was prodigal of so much unaccustomed tenderness that Fanny's suspicions were at once awakened. In his clumsy fashion he thought it a master stroke to tell her that he had gone to the circus on the previous evening for the sole pleasure of looking at his mistress from a distance. He entirely ignored all those proofs of weariness which he had far too often given Fanny in the past, and was ready to convince himself that a woman in love can have the wool pulled over her eyes in the crudest fashion. But his kindness worried his mistress far more than the rebuffs to which she had grown used. His clumsiness at times verged on the ridiculous. Much of his charm was due to his attitude of complete indifference where love was concerned. The apathy with which he could take without even pretending to give in return could be actually attractive. It was apt to be shot through with an occasional access of violent passion which made up for all that had gone before, making it possible for her to endure the rapidly ensuing mood of bitterness, and the sight of his face suddenly withdrawn behind a curtain of self-disgust.

How false his voice sounded when he allowed himself to go so far as to say that he was *"longing"* for the Quai Debilly! The stupid creature really believed that it was impossible for love to be clear-sighted. He forgot (if he had ever known) that though the one who is loved may know nothing of the other who loves, the reverse is never true. Fanny knew the youth on whom her whole happiness, her very life, depended, far better than she knew herself. She was too weather-wise a sailor, had too often studied, when they met, her lover's every gesture and every look, not immediately to smell out deception when it came her way. In his case absence of love meant absence of knowledge. Indifference is blind. Why should he want to start coming again to the Quai Debilly? The thought of Colombe as a possible explanation had not yet entered her mind, either because it did not occur to her that so young a girl could please a man in that way (not to mention the fact that she found her gawky and plain), or because the idea of Fabien really in love would have been intolerable to her. She must, however, have been getting "warm" when she said to him:

"You can come to the house quite safely on Saturday. Donald won't be back until late. He's dining at Versailles with the Princess . . . and the next day he's off again."

Instinctively she avoided saying anything more about this projected trip of her husband, which in point of fact closely concerned Colombe. A more attentive lover would have noticed how she was lighting cigarette after cigarette and throwing each away almost unsmoked: the way in which she kept on flicking the ash off with her finger. As a rule she took "a perfect age"—as Fabien said—"to get out of the room," but tonight she seemed all eagerness to be alone. Far from letting this worry him, he found in it a reason for rejoicing. He could not go on much longer aping a tenderness he did not feel, and found himself caddishly blaming her—poor thing!—for the necessity he was under to play a part.

The Weakling and the Enemy

He let her leave first. Only when she had got a good start on him did he emerge from the house in the rue Visconti. Instead of going straight back to his hotel, he crossed the Seine at a brisk pace and walked for a while along the railings of the Tuileries gardens. The gates at this hour had been already closed, so that he was shut out from communion with the trees which lent a note of beauty to the misty emptiness within. That very morning he had sent in his resignation to the Director of the École des Chartes. In two days' time he would be seeing Colombe again. Thus he had taken the first step to freedom and happiness. To gauge the extent of his love he no longer had to imagine that Colombe was dead, nor yet to conjure up the image of that last letter she might have written to him. After every tryst in the rue Visconti his passion for the girl increased, drawing strength from the feelings of disgust which Fanny woke in him. In what way did the young fool imagine that marriage would differ from what he had known already? What sort of a dream was it that he entertained of a sensuality made one with chastity? It was not yet quite dark, and he felt a little shock of surprise to find that the sky above the Place de la Concorde could be so beautiful, brushed in, as it were, for the express purpose of serving as a background to it. He felt no need of companionship. If, at that moment, he had run across Maïnz, he would have avoided him. The fullness of his heart sufficed. In the rue de la Paix he was conscious of the silent invitation lurking in the faces of shopgirls disgorged from the various buildings. His wild pigeon, he thought, would put up scarcely any resistance. He had only to beckon and she would come.

At last the day dawned when he was to see the girl. He

started the afternoon by having his hair cut, after which he returned to his hotel and ran up the stairs, whistling. Fanny was waiting for him in his room. She was sitting on the bed. Her furs gave her a thick and padded appearance, and she was wearing a veil. He tried in vain to keep his temper. He had not been expecting her, and this sort of thing was not playing the game. There was nothing he so much disliked as meeting her at times other than those of their prearranged trysts in the rue Visconti. . . . There would be trouble with the manager.

"And I'd planned it as such a pleasant surprise for you! You were so sweet to me last time!"

He heard the ache in her words, but not the irony. It was just like women all over, he grumbled: the more one gives, the more they want. He walked up and down the tiny room, the ceiling of which he could have touched by stretching his hand. He began gesticulating in a sudden burst of southern exuberance. She, meanwhile, remained motionless on the bed, watching him. Her passivity got on his nerves. He told her that she must go.

"Come on, get out!"

What he meant was, "Leave this room," but she made a pretense of believing that he intended this to be a final break, and began to whine.

"But where am I to go, Fabien?"

She was at the end of her tether, within measurable distance of complete collapse.

"You no longer believe a word I say. No one ever does believe people who say they wish they were dead."

"We're dead already," he replied.

She tried to turn the whole thing into a joke.

"I must say, my dear, you've got a very odd idea of love!

The Weakling and the Enemy

Those who tried to make love a crime were rightly regarded as the enemies of the human race. . . . If only I could convince you that the only way of loving is to avoid all these complicated feelings, these dramas, these metaphysical subtleties. . . ."

"Oh, do for once look at things straight! If you hadn't met me that day in Venice, you would have been dead by this time!"

He had lost all control of himself. He told her, not once but again and again, that, but for him, love would have killed her. None but fools and hypocrites maintained that it was only religion that had given love its power to destroy, that, but for religion, passion would be nothing but unalloyed delight. As though the flesh was not perfectly capable, unaided, of distilling poison! Though, as a rule, he hated any suspicion of rhetoric, he added:

"Go out into the streets, into the promenades of music halls, into the brothels, and see what this beautiful 'love' you're always talking about can make of human beings!"

She protested that what he was referring to wasn't love at all. He agreed, but only to argue that what she called love produced precisely the same fruit. It didn't need God to interfere. Concupiscence alone could set the world in a blaze. He made no attempt to moderate his language, but went on to describe with gloating delight the hideous old age of women who have lived only for the pleasures of the body—Circes made desperate by the realization that they can no longer turn men into swine. It was no arbitrary pronouncement of the Church that had conferred this frightful pre-eminence on the sin of sexual vice and sensual self-indulgence. Once let human beings set their feet upon that slippery slope and there was no stopping their headlong descent.

The Weakling and the Enemy

And so he talked on, pressing his face to the window, not seeing the prostrate figure on the bed, though he could hear her panting breath. Suddenly he was overwhelmed by a sense of shame because he had brought God into this discussion. It was from habit only that he was trotting out these noble sentiments. If he had not wanted Colombe he could have put up with Fanny. It was a young girl—and not the Infinite Majesty—who was estranging him from his former mistress.

Like many women who are quite incapable of putting two and two together, or of arguing rationally, she kept on repeating, either because she had not heard, or had entirely failed to grasp, what Fabien was saying:

"If it wasn't for these morbid scruples of yours, darling, you *would* love me, and there would be joy for you in that love."

"You poor, demented creature, *can't* you see that if I don't wash my hands of you, it's for one reason and one reason only —because I feel that I am responsible for your immortal soul. I wonder whether you've got the slightest idea what it means to be responsible for another person's immortal soul? What binds us together is the sin that we have jointly committed. I can't acquiesce in your eternal damnation. We must sink or swim together. . . . But I don't suppose that a single word of what I'm saying makes sense to you."

Once again he relapsed into silence. He was filled with a sense of self-loathing because if, once upon a time, he really had felt some such scruple, really had believed that he had no right to concentrate upon his own salvation to the exclusion of hers, it was equally true today that he didn't give a hang for Fanny or for the destiny of her immortal soul. Of what had formerly been in him an excessive sensitivity of conscience he retained, now, nothing but the vocabulary. That his sin had been joyless did not alter the fact that, because of it, he had become diminished in moral stature, impoverished and hard.

Fanny got up, went over to him, put her arms round his neck, and moaned in heartbroken accents:

"Oh, *don't* tell me that's the only reason that you have remained faithful to me!"

Because she had been a constant first-nighter, a phrase of modish theatrical jargon came easily to her lips (on anybody else's it would have sounded comic):

"Ah, Fabien, do not be false to our love!"

He gave a mirthless laugh and shrugged his shoulders. She switched on the light, and they gazed at one another with eyes that were eloquent of nothing but violence and death: she, desolate with weeping, old and defeated; he, no whit diminished in his vigor by their acrid argument. His youth seemed actually to have gained something of radiance from the devastation of the storm that had been raging between them, like a tree whose leaves look all the greener and more brilliant for the rain. . . . Fanny was tidying her hair before the mirror, fastening her veil. She must be going because they had a dinner party that evening. In Fabien's mind there was nothing at this moment but the thought of Colombe, and he said with the gayest of gay intonations:

"I'll be round as soon as I've changed."

She turned toward him, utterly dumbfounded. How could he *dream* of dining at the Quai Debilly after such a scene? She noticed his expression of mingled embarrassment and expectation. With assumed indifference she said:

"You'd much better wait a few hours. Donald's going away

tomorrow for a month. He *says* it's because he's got to take Colombe back to her mother, but actually he's going to meet Leda Southers. . . ."

"Is Colombe leaving, then?"

Fabien could not help raising his voice. Fanny appeared to interpret his cry as indicative of joy.

"Yes, you spoiled child: father and daughter are going to leave the coast clear. You'll be able, once more, to treat the Quai Debilly as your home."

He went with her to the door.

"Perhaps," he said uncertainly, "I'll look in for a moment round about ten, just to ask your forgiveness for my ill-temper."

Fanny went down the dark staircase, her face turned toward her lover, who was standing looking over the banisters. In the car she forced herself to gaze straight and firmly at this new uprush of pain, this sudden onset of agonizing jealousy. She was like a newly awakened sleeper who, when the shutters are thrown open, has to accustom his eyes to the blinding sunlight.

12

FABIEN must have realized his danger, because, having dressed with the intention of dining at the Quai Debilly, in spite of Fanny's protest, he dared not take the risk, but wandered about in the mist that hung about between the parapet and the trees of the deserted river bank. He would not go up until he had seen the lights flash on behind the curtains of the drawing-room windows. He had an instinctive awareness of the peril he was running, but could think of nothing but Colombe and her impending departure. Once she had gone he would fall again into the old rut, would find himself face to face with Fanny for ever and ever. From then on his life would be completely empty. But there was still this one evening left, and he had made up his mind to take the chance it offered.

They must have finished dinner by this time. He entered the house, but was terrified by the reflection of his haggard face in the hall mirror, and stopped for a moment to straighten his tie. Fanny was not in the large drawing room, and his entrance passed unnoticed. Colombe was not there either. He hunted for her in vain through all the other rooms, but found no trace of her until he reached the small room furnished with lacquer, where he had got drunk one evening on sweet wine. He came to a dead stop outside the door, his heart beating, because he had recognized the voices of Cyrus Bargues and Colombe.

The Weakling and the Enemy

"*Actually,* in a month's time all the women will have had their hair cut; you see if I'm not right. Do let me cut yours, *dear* Colombe. A balletmaster can turn his hand to anything. I should hate you to go before I had seen you looking like a young and sexless god with a head of cropped curls. . . . It'll be so *screamingly* funny to play a trick on the others. The melancholy stallion will look more melancholy than ever."

Fabien trembled because he heard Colombe say: "Oh, *he* doesn't bother about *me.* We all know why *he's* here, don't we?"

"For you, darling. Why, he just *gobbles* you up with his eyes . . . besides, he has talked to me about you. . . ."

"That's not true, and you only say it because you want to make me angry. You don't believe, do you, that I care what a horrible creature like that thinks? No, please don't tell me what he said. I'm sure it was something beastly."

Fabien could imagine the childish mouth all puckered up to spit out that final word "beastly." But Cyrus was protesting:

"No, really you're wrong. *Actually* he's terribly good-looking."

"I'm not talking about his appearance."

"That's the only thing about him that matters, Colombe, dear. . . ."

"What *did* he say about me? Something awful, I'm sure. Do tell me, Cyrus."

"If you want me to answer your question, go and fetch the scissors. It really will be great fun. You see if it isn't. You will feel them cold against your neck. I can hear the sound of them cutting through that dense young forest of yours . . . cro . . . cro . . . cro. We'll let the melancholy stallion sweep up the fallen locks."

189

The Weakling and the Enemy

"How silly you are, Cyrus: you're quite the silliest boy I've ever met. You don't honestly think, do you, that I mind what the melancholy stallion said about me? And, by the way, why do you call him a stallion? Isn't a stallion a thoroughbred horse? I don't think *he's* got much breeding . . . he's more like a country lout. . . . Look how thick my hair is, and I've got nothing but embroidery scissors."

"I've seen scissors of all sizes in Fanny's dressing room. Come along, Colombe. Nobody will disturb us there, and we can achieve the transformation at our leisure. I can work miracles. A dancer is possessed of the divine fire. At this moment you're nothing but a little girl—but you're going to be turned into a young Bacchus. You'll enchant not only the melancholy stallion but all those who find delight in ambiguities and uncertainties and the mingling of the sexes."

"There's something awfully odd about you, Cyrus. Do you know what I think when I look into your little burning eyes— that you're possessed by a devil!"

Fabien heard the sound of their mingled laughter, followed by low whispering and the noise of a door being cautiously opened. They were going into the dressing room. Without stopping to think, he followed them, and entered just as Colombe, already seated, was obediently bending her neck. She got up, looking very pale. Turning to Cyrus Bargues, Fabien pointed to the door. Anger made him dumb, but his lower lip was trembling, and he gripped the dancer's arm so tightly that the latter made a face.

"What a *brute* you are, Dézaymeries!"

Fabien pushed him outside, shut the door and mopped his forehead with his handkerchief. The look that he turned on

The Weakling and the Enemy

Colombe was both tender and fearful, so tender that the girl imparted a tone of gentleness to the insolent words that she had made up her mind to fling at him.

"What right have you to interfere?"

He answered in a low voice but with the authority of a lover: "I didn't want him to cut your hair."

She smiled like a schoolgirl remembering her history lesson, and said:

"You would rather see me dead at your feet than cropped? ..."

Then she stopped short and her eyebrows drew together into a funny little frown.

"Since you're going away, Colombe, you must forget all the things that have been said against me in this house. . . . The people here are just a lot of swine. . . ."

She raised her eyes and looked him straight in the face.

"Doesn't that include you, too?"

He seemed abashed.

"It does," he stammered; "but at least I know it. *They've* no idea of the depths to which they have fallen. . . ."

"So much the better for them!"

"You *can't* know. Some day I'll tell you. I'm a miserable sinner, Colombe. Do you hear what I say? A sinner."

With a sad smile, and as though repeating a lesson, she said: "A miserable sinner."

"Yes, Colombe, a *miserable* sinner, and a bit of a hypocrite too."

She saw such a look of shame in the dark, virile face that she made as though to raise her hands—perhaps with the intention of taking it between them, of drawing it to her—then let them fall to her sides. Stunned, her arms hanging, the child stood

there, motionless beneath the crude light of the enamelled dressing room which was filled with the untidiness of clothes hurriedly changed. Pots of make-up and various brushes lay all over
the table. A bottle of scent with its cork out was slowly evap-
orating. A thermometer was floating on the soapy water of the
bath. The place was so small and so cumbered that they were
standing very close together. Colombe, looking as though she
had no resistance left in her, said:

"What do you want me to do?"

"Take this sponge and wipe the rouge from your cheeks," he
said, as though that were the most pressing need of the moment.

"There!"

"And now the black round your eyes."

"It's done!"

"And the red from your lips."

"What next?"

She obeyed him like someone walking in her sleep. He asked
her whether she liked being with her mother in Brussels.

"Mamma is the kind of person you would like," she answered, as though she were familiar with all the tastes of this
young man, to whom she had spoken only twice before. "The
idea that I'm with my guardian makes her wild! I wish you
could read her letters. She's afraid I shall learn bad habits here.
She's glad, of course, that my guardian should take an interest
in me, but she's worried about my soul. . . ."

"Don't leave her, Colombe—not until I come and fetch you."

"Fetch me?"

She smiled at him, her face transfigured, cleansed, fresh. The
only color in her cheeks now came from the young blood flow-
ing in her veins, from the love rising in her heart. Her eyelids

fluttered as with a sign of assent. She scarcely more than whispered her address, but Fabien remembered it. They said no more, but stood there looking at one another. They did not know that, at that very moment, Fanny, to whom Cyrus had murmured, "If you want to see two lovebirds, go along to your dressing room," had risen from her chair and was coming toward them. They did not hear the rustling of her dress. She pushed open the door. The two young people were not in one another's arms when she came in, were not even touching, but as they stood facing one another, love blazed in their faces, so that it dazzled her. For a moment she closed her eyes, then, with a smile, turning to Colombe, she said:

"Your guardian's waiting for you, my dear."

She took her by the hand and led her away. Fabien sighed. There would be no dramatics—at the most, perhaps, a scene. It would not be difficult for him to defend himself. Colombe and he had been doing nothing wrong. He avoided going back to the drawing room, but got his overcoat and left the house.

He leaned over the parapet and looked at the river. The surface was popply, and the reflected lights were broken. His eyes took in the bare branches, the sleeping houses, the stars. A clear road was opening through his darkness. He knew now the way he must take, but it would be rough with briars and underbrush and torn roots. Back in his room, he prayed—at long last he could pluck up courage to do that! Then he lay down, not as heretofore, like a corpse, but curled up on one side, with his two hands pressed to his heart, as though they were holding something in, though what he did not know.

In the very early hours of the next morning someone threw the door open very suddenly and turned on the light. Sitting up in bed, he recognized Cyrus Bargues, who was still in evening dress.

"My dear, something *frightful's* happened. You must get up at once! Fanny's gone and swallowed a whole lot of opium and digitalin and heaven knows what else. I gather that there is still hope, but she won't let the doctor touch her unless you come. . . ."

His eyes never left Fabien all the while that the young man was hunting for his clothes.

"Women with a taste for suicide, my dear, are upsetting only if you attach importance to what happens to them. My own view is that it is best to leave them to their fate. Everyone has a right to die if he wants to, don't you agree? *Actually,* death usually *does* simplify matters so much for the survivors. Take your own case. . . ."

"Shut up, for heaven's sake! I don't want to hear another word from you. You give me the horrors! Is the car there?"

"It's waiting. I *adore* you when you're angry. But you can be terribly *rough,* you know. I really felt quite a *worm* yesterday evening. You're nothing but a great brute, really, but then all interesting people are."

The car slipped through the dawn. All the way along the river Fabien felt angry with himself for being so acutely aware of the crisp, sad beauty of the empty city, while Cyrus Bargues sat at his side dreamily quoting:

> *L'aurore grelottante en robe rose et verte*
> *S'avançait lentement sur la Seine déserte.*

The front door was half open. Donald Larsen, his shirt front rumpled, his tie askew, was on the lookout for their arrival. He told them not to make a noise. Colombe, he said, was asleep, and on no account must she know what had happened. At the door of the bedroom he took Fabien by the arm, leaned with his enormous bulk till he was so close that the young man could smell his breath, which reeked of tobacco and spirits, and said:

"She's *got* to live—see?"

He added that he couldn't put off his own or the girl's departure. He made it quite clear that if Fanny were to die he would hold Fabien responsible.

"She's *got* to live!"

Fabien uttered no protest. The man filled him with terror and loathing. He looked like a cat with its ears laid back, and spitting. The sound of Fanny struggling for breath on the other side of the door could not take his mind from another room where Colombe lay sleeping.

1 3

No, don't draw the curtains, and don't come any closer. Sit down over there in that beam of sunlight. It's enough for me if I can just look at you."

Fabien, from the other side of the room, could see the thin face among the pillows. His thoughts turned to the woman with whom he had once travelled across Europe. He could feel her eyes upon him. They affected him like a physical contact. He begged her, now that she was well again, to get up.

"No," she said; "leave me at least *that* consolation, to lie still, to doze, to sleep. I'm going to be sensible, Fabien, truly I am. I was hateful, I was grotesque—that especially; but you don't have to worry now. I have learned at last to wait patiently until the end comes . . . but that is all I can do—just wait. Please realize that. I saw Heinemann, the dealer, this morning: you know whom I mean, don't you? He's going to sell everything I've got here, bit by bit. It'll be a slow business and will last as long as I shall. I like to think of ending my days in a completely empty room. . . . But one thing you must promise —to come every day and just sit in that chair for a few minutes. I want to learn again how to love you as I loved you once in your mother's room. . . . I think it was you, probably, who made me realize, in those days, how satisfying a refuge a shut room could be, a bed, with the monotonous ticking of a clock and the whisper of a dying fire, with shadows moving on the walls and ceiling. Do you remember how you used to revel in your childish ailments? No more games in an icy playground, you used to say, no more masters, no more little school friends."

Fabien remembered the nights when he had kept his mouth tight shut so as not to cough, when he had lain for what seemed an infinity in an uncomfortable position so as to avoid waking his mother and making her anxious. When the doctor had leaned down to listen to his heart his beard had smelled of toilet vinegar. He had been able to see the man's scalp as though through a magnifying glass. The Christmas Annual for '87 had contained *Little Lord Fauntleroy,* and the one for '94, *Moustique.* There had been other stories as well, two of which, he recollected, had been called *Chan-Ook* and *Maltaverne.*

When he found himself once again in the street he felt as though he had returned from some distant land, bringing the old Fanny with him. She seemed emptied now of all desires. She no longer wanted him. How strange that was! So far there had been no answer to the long letter he had written to Colombe. Her long silence should have surprised him, but he had had no time for wondering. He awaited her reply without impatience. His lovely dream was on the point of becoming a rather formidable reality. Should he say anything about Colombe to Madame Dézaymeries? What was the point in telling her that the girl's father was Fanny's second husband, or that she was a natural child? Madame Dézaymeries would consent to no compromise with her standards. Prejudices can be overcome, but not principles, and Fabien knew that in his mother's case, what the world called prejudices were founded in reason and solidly built on foundations which, to her mind, showed no crack. He was amazed to detect within himself no movement of rebellion. Often, now, he let his imagination dwell on the child who would be his son, a child with Larsen's china-blue eyes and Larsen's complexion, which looked as though the blood were oozing through the skin. He must, all the same, make *some* approach to the subject, must indicate, when next he wrote to his mother, that he was contemplating marriage. But his letters were always so short. . . . And, suddenly, he blushed. He who, as a child, had never been guilty of a lie, had not dared to tell his mother that he had left the École des Chartes, had, in fact, quite shamelessly given her details of a purely imaginary success in the quarterly examination. . . . Away with the memory of such cowardice! . . . He must try to concentrate his thoughts on his wild pigeon. . . .

He was obsessed, too, by worry of a different kind, though he did his best to see it only as a rather bizarre oddity. Was Fanny really and truly cured of him? Did she sincerely see him only as the small boy he once had been, or was she playing a deep game? "What does it matter?" he said to himself. "The important thing is that you are free at last. No need, now that you are tied no longer to that aging body, to worry about being a dirty little beast." But there were times, especially at night, as he lay in his lonely bed, when he found his mind dwelling on the thought of the body which once he had so loathed. What is it in our nature that urges us to repeat gestures that used to make us feel physically sick? It is impossible to judge of the damage done until the storm has passed. Now that Fanny had broken loose, had withdrawn into herself and made the great renunciation, the poor young man could turn his eye inward and mark the incurable wound from which the blood still oozed.

The Weakling and the Enemy

Accustomed, ever since the age of seven, to making a meticulous examination of his conscience, to the workings of casuistry in its most subtle forms, he was completely ignorant of the crude mechanism of what the world calls love, of an emotion which can so order matters that an abhorred mistress whom we long to throw overboard can, quite suddenly—if she takes the initiative and, without a word of warning, anticipate our contemplated desertion—become precious in our eyes. When that happens a sudden hunger treads hard upon the heels of our satiety. Fabien believed himself to be precisely as he had been before embarking on a life of sin. He was utterly unaware of the new man within him who lived subject to a new law. That was why, when the existence of this stranger was revealed, the fact of it struck like a thunderbolt.

He had come one day, rather earlier than usual, to the Quai Debilly. The nurse asked him to wait until Fanny should be ready, and he sat in the empty drawing room, a prey to impatience. He thought that he could best rid himself of his obsession by showing Fanny some sign of tenderness, by testing her, by putting temptation in her path.

Consequently it was with considerable nervousness that he approached the bed.

She pushed him away.

"No, Fabien, no: sit down in your usual chair. I like it so much better when you can only guess what I look like."

All the time that she was speaking in her husky voice, he was saying to himself: "She wouldn't be afraid of my seeing her if she had really stopped loving me."

"At least let me hold your hand, Fanny."

She stretched out her small, bare hand, but it no longer

trembled in his own. While he faintly pressed it, she went on talking in that voice that invalids always use when they are interested in nothing but themselves:

"I had a little chicken this morning, and I actually enjoyed it."

He increased the pressure, and she gently withdrew her hand before proceeding:

"How odd it all is. . . . After that other time I tried to kill myself I never really regained the zest of living, but now, when I'm a great deal older, it has suddenly come back!"

"Look at me, Fanny! You haven't once looked at me since I came into the room. . . ."

He remembered how, in the old days, it had been she, always, who had used such words to him.

Very gently she said:

"That was on purpose, my dear. I must get used to not seeing you. . . . I saw enough to tell me how you are. . . . You ought to get away into the country . . . you're not looking at all well."

"I don't want to leave you alone."

"I think the cure is complete, Fabien. But I shan't know for certain until you have been away from me for some time. . . ."

A hint of the old chiding note which had marked their former quarrels crept into his voice as he replied:

"I know why you want to send me away!"

She flashed him a questioning look, and he went on:

"You may as well admit that it's because of Colombe. You want to punish me. . . ."

Once more she stared at him, then struggled into a sitting position and covered her eyes and mouth with her two hands.

The Weakling and the Enemy

Between the splayed fingers there came a sound, but whether it was a laugh or a sob he could not tell.

"You dare mention that name to me. Oh, what a little f-fool you are!" (She stammered slightly over the word.) "And, anyhow, you're entirely wrong, because I don't care *that* for your Colombe, especially now when I realize that you are just like the rest of them. . . . Oh, Fabien, Fabien! there was a time when I thought of you as belonging to a different race. You may be a pious little fanatic on the surface, but underneath you're just the same sort of beast—yes, I mean that—the same sort of beast as all those others who start wanting to get their victim back into their clutches the moment it's stopped yowling!"

How truly had this old purveyor of love summed up love's mechanism! Brooding there over the gawky youth before her, her astute and knowing glance fixed on his thin cheeks and passion-worn face, she said again:

"Just like the rest of them! Just like the rest of them!"

He sat in a species of silent stupor, he who had been used to causing pain, not suffering it. At last he stuttered out:

"All the same, you tried to kill yourself because of me, because of her—you can't deny that!"

She broke in on him:

"That put the lid on it! Yes, I suppose my suicide would have been a feather in your cap. . . . How you'd hate it if I told you it had been just a put-up job! But don't worry; you're perfectly right. The sight of you and her together was more than I could stand. . . . What a fool I was! I wanted at all costs to tear that picture out of my mind, but how thankful, how terribly thankful, I am that I failed! I can be at peace now. I know that I'm stronger than you are. What does it matter now if your Colombe has been sent back to her convent for another two years! What, didn't you know? Then she's not as sharp as I thought her, though of course Donald never leaves anything to chance, and I expect he's taken pretty good care to have a watch kept on her letters. But what does it matter? I said to myself: 'In two years' time he'll have forgotten all about her!' And I thought I knew men! I should have said—in two days!"

She was expecting him to utter some sort of protest, to invoke the absent girl; but he said nothing.

Their eyes met. The young man she saw before her seemed to be a complete stranger, a lover who now, after all these months, was really suffering because of her. There were tears in his eyes, and she almost felt inclined, for the first time in her life, to feel sorry for him. But her pity would not have been quite sincere, for there would have been in it a hint of that satisfaction we all feel when we think, "Well, it's his turn now, poor wretch!"

"Forgive me, my dear, but you really are too ridiculous. I poisoned your existence with my threats of suicide. Then, at last, I actually did something about it. I failed, and suddenly I woke up, free at last, though not of my fondness, if that's any comfort to you. And all through that terrible time, when I really thought that everything was over, life seemed sweeter to me than ever before. You can't have any idea what it is like to see sunlight on a window when one is conscious of it only at a great distance and through gathering shadows. Yes, I was free at last and saved! Lying here in a sort of animal stupor, I took stock of my madness. Thanks to my drowsiness, to the numbness that paralyzed all my physical senses, I could sit in judgment on myself. What a terrible injury I had done you! 'He must go back to his mother,' I said to myself, looking at the misery in your face. 'You must try to have for him the same innocent love as when he was a little boy.' It seemed to me almost easy to do that. I once heard someone say that the wisdom of old age consists in being able to see the difference between pleasure and love."

He listened to her, biting his short mustache, worrying at it with his fingers. At last, in a hard and arrogant tone, he put a question:

"Am I the only person you allow to come and see you?"

"Why do you ask me that?"

"Because I know what you are. You can't live without some man . . . you never have been able to. If you're turning your back on me now, it's because you've found somebody better worth your while!"

She was so taken aback that for a moment she made no answer. To herself she murmured: "It's hardly credible!" She stretched her hand to her bedside lamp and switched it on. Then, tilting back the dark silk shade, she lay silently staring at the stranger in her room, with his tousled hair, his shoes, and the bottoms of his trousers caked with mud, a lunatic look in his eyes. She remembered all those many times when she had praised his looks, and he had said: "I'm just like any mule driver you might meet on the roads round my home." Yes, that was precisely what he *was* like—a young mule driver.

"You really must be going out of your mind, Fabien! Whom else *should* I see? I have given orders that no one else is to be admitted except you and Cyrus Bargues. But his season at Covent Garden begins in a week's time, and he's off on Friday. Besides, Cyrus Bargues, I ask you!"

"Who's your doctor?"

"Why not add, my concierge, my postman! I've had just about as much as I can stand. Go and get some air into your lungs. I'm still pretty weak, you know."

Hesitatingly he went to the door, and stopped. In the light of the lamp he could see her hand fumbling at the sheet. She must have turned away for he caught the glint of her tumbled hair. He used to tell her that it was far too yellow, but at this moment all he wanted was to plunge his face in it.

Suddenly he heard her laugh, and asked her what it was she found so amusing.

"Oh, you're still there, are you?"

"Why are you laughing?"

"Listen to me, Fabien, and don't be angry. I was thinking how you used to reproach me for alienating you from God. I shall be pretty invalidish for the next few weeks, and then it will be Easter. Thérèse is waiting for you. . . . You're not going on playing the part of the prodigal son, are you?"

She heard the door of her room slam, and, a few moments later, the door leading to the stairs. Did she feel sorry that she could not run after him? She took up a hand mirror and looked long at her temples, her neck, her eyelids, her cheeks—stroking them with her fingers.

1 4

HE WALKED along the street with his overcoat open and his hat pulled down over his eyes, and as he went he said to himself: "She's right: it's never once occurred to you that the road lies open, that there's nothing now to stop you from finding your way back into the life of grace." This forgetfulness showed him, far more clearly than would have done the sense of having committed a fearful crime, how far he had fallen. Had he lost his faith? Of what use is faith if it is not lived? What value has an intellectual system, a theory of the universe, be it ever so perfunctory, if one does not guide one's conduct by its rules? "You're a corpse, you're beginning to stink already: there's not the slightest hint in you of any desire to rise again, nothing but this maniacal craving, this longing to be convinced that you still exercise an abominable influence over Fanny. You loathe her, but you won't give up the power of life and death. You're just like all the other swine—only worse!"

Fabien Dézaymeries did not see that in one essential point he differed from the majority of his fellows, in the fact that he was clear-sighted, lucid, and could gaze without flinching into his own heart. The scrupulous care that he had given, since his childhood days, to the examination of his motives, to the confession of the tiniest impure thought; the readiness he had always shown to blacken himself rather than run the risk of leaving undisclosed the smallest blemish (he had always been terrified of concealing a sin), kept him now from all danger of resting content with deceptive appearances. Most lovers would have gloried in their loyalty to an old mistress, would have waxed sentimental and self-satisfied over the realization that they were more capable than they had ever thought they could be of a love that was deep and sincere. He saw through all such illusions, and plumbed the hateful depths of his own nature where lurked the monstrous feelings that were not even sure of their own identity, such dark regions as those in which two young women may suddenly be forced to realize that what they took for friendship is really passion. He saw now just how much rancorous hatred there was in this suddenly renewed craving for Fanny. How terribly youth can torture itself! It complains because it is fated to drag after itself a huddle of chained slaves whose weight lies heavy on its movements, yet, no sooner is it freed from them than it bewails the absence of those very victims who once gave living proof of its power.

Only when he reached his bedroom door did he awake from this long process of meditation. Among the letters waiting for him he recognized an envelope addressed in his own writing. It contained the letter he had written to Colombe on the very day of her departure, and here it was, returned to him. Although he had been careful to put his address on a corner of the envelope, somebody, who could not have been Colombe, had opened it and read its rather foolish sentiments. How far he felt this evening from all those sugar-sweet protestations! He was not in the least tempted to make even a gesture that might have the effect of averting an obstructive fate. He knew that the battle for

The Weakling and the Enemy

Colombe was lost, but knew too that it was in his own heart that he had been defeated. No external obstacles could have stood against his love, but he could find now, within himself, not the tiniest trace of that small and still-born creature. A girl, still scarcely more than a child, had been the means of revealing to him the existence of carnal delights that might be blessed and sanctified, of caresses from which the shadowy angels would not avert their gaze; but he realized now that this young and charming human being, the only one of her kind whom he had ever known, had been the occasion rather than the object of that great surge of feeling.

The other letter he dared not open, though the neat handwriting was dear to him. It was the same that, in the old days, he had spelled out on the "excuse cards" which had followed hard on the heels of his childhood illnesses, the cards that he would have to hand up to the headmaster: *Madame Dézaymeries begs the Abbé Bernard to be so very kind as to excuse her son Fabien, who has been confined to the house with influenza.* It was the same as that which he had covered with tears and kisses during prep. all through that month of October when he and Joseph had been sent to school as boarders because their mother had stayed on in the country. He had no doubt that this letter which he dared not open had been written, as all her letters to him were, in the belief that it was addressed to a frank and honest boy, to the young Christian who now lay murdered, though she clung obstinately to the conviction that he was still alive. It was true that each time he had gone home she had suffered cruelly because he seemed a stranger, because his voice sounded as though it were reaching her from a distance, because a hot fire glowed in his shifty glances, a fire that was not the sacred flame which she had kindled in his heart. But scarcely had he gone away again than the old lady unconsciously set herself to revivify the ghost of the innocent child who had gone to sleep each night with his two hands, linked by a rosary, crossed upon his breast.

He glanced nervously at the first few lines. No, *this* letter was not addressed to that pious, docile boy. For two months now his own letters had been so short, their tone so dry (especially since he had lied to her about the École des Chartes), that the old lady could not but feel a certain foreboding. "My dear son: I cannot recognize your voice in the words you send me. If your letters were not in your writing I should think they came from a stranger. There was a time when you used to confide in your old mother. I know exactly when that stopped—it was after your first year at school. All the same, up to a month or two ago you did at least tell me about the little events of your life. But now it is only too obvious that you are impatient to get quit of a tiresome duty. Don't you think I can tell that from the shortness of the lines, from their being more widely spaced, from the manifest tricks you've been reduced to in order to cover four pages in the quickest possible time? Someone who knows you said to me the other day: 'When a child no longer confides in his mother, you can be quite sure that there is more on his mind than he wants to tell.' I protested. I reminded the good Father of the notorious Dézaymeries reticence. My poor husband was just the same, and never really unburdened himself. . . . Still, I am not sufficiently convinced myself to be able to reassure our saintly friend. I have never dared to tell him that you refused to communicate on the anniversary of Joseph's death. . . . My dearest boy, I have been thinking a great deal and praying a great deal. I suppose it was partly a mother's pride that led me to think that you are different from other men, that evil is powerless to touch you. . . . If I am wrong, forgive me for making a foolhardy judgment. If my fear is justified, where should you find a surer refuge than in a mother whose love for you is so great that it may well be a cause of offense in the eyes of a jealous God? But Easter is not far off, and on the Thursday in Holy Week we shall, as we always have done every year, kneel together at the Lord's table, and my child in his weakness will take the bread that gives strength. . . ."

Fabien found it impossible to read further. He crumpled the letter in his hand, and began to walk up and down the low, dark room. His eyes were like those of some vicious animal. Could he have seen them in a mirror he would have been terrified. "Oh, why can't she leave me alone!" he muttered. "I'm old enough in all conscience, and my troubles are my own concern. . . . If she really expects to see me at Easter . . ." It was inconceivable that he should go home. What possible excuse could he make for not taking Communion? He would be quite incapable of enduring in silence his mother's searching inquiries. The very thought of the questions she would ask him made him grind his teeth. But what carried most weight with him was the need he felt not to leave Paris without being certain that the other woman was still at his mercy.

"All the same, you don't love her, and you know it." So much the worse, then. There was no use in trying to probe *that* mystery. There was nothing he could do to fight against the urgent demand of his whole being that the former slave should not be allowed to escape him, still less that she should put her neck beneath a new yoke. A new yoke? At that very moment, while he was pacing his room, she was probably laughing at him with some man whom most certainly she would not keep sitting at a safe distance. Who was that unknown for whose sake she had been waiting in Venice, who had failed to turn up? Fabien had never bothered to find out his name. . . .

He took his coat and hat and rushed out into the street. At first he walked, then, mad with impatience, hailed a taxi and had himself driven to the Place de l'Alma. He strode along the dark quay until he reached Fanny's house. A faint light showed behind her bedroom windows—the light of the reading lamp. Perhaps, after all, there was no one with her. She couldn't be asleep at eight o'clock in the evening. Entering, he plucked up courage to question the concierge, who thought, though she couldn't be sure, that Madame was alone. . . .

He hung about for some time between the parapet and the trees of the deserted quay.

Next day he made an immense effort not to ring at her door until three o'clock. He had decided to adopt an attitude of feigned indifference, as though on her alone it depended whether their relationship should remain unchanged, or whether they should draw their lives to a new pattern, see their existences in a new light. Nothing should stand in the way of her finding in him a Fabien drained of all the desire that she no longer felt: nothing should stand in the way of his finding in her the mournful charm of the fugitive from an outworn emotion. From the moment of his arrival he showed a gentle humility toward the woman to whom, in the days of their love, he had been hard and arrogant. He made it clear that he longed to be admitted to every trivial moment in the life of a mistress about whose movements he had formerly shown a lack of curiosity which had driven her almost into the arms of death.

"Who brought you that lilac?"

"I shouldn't have many flowers in this room if I depended on you to bring them. . . . It was Coco and the Princess. They looked in yesterday after you'd gone. The Princess is really kindness itself. Did I tell you that she's taking me with her into the country the day after tomorrow? I'm going to finish my convalescence at Cap Ferrat. She's got one of the loveliest gardens on that part of the coast. . . ."

Not a word did he utter. Whatever he did he must not show what he was feeling. She kept her gaze fixed upon the gawky, carelessly dressed, emaciated and bony youth with the bilious-looking eyes, and to herself she said: "A mule driver." How strange it is to look at a face that we have loved when we love it no longer. Only a short while ago Fanny had been dying for the sake of this same mouth, of these same eyes, which had a glint in them when they smiled. She remembered the Sunday (only a fortnight gone) when she had felt that she would never stop crying, when, on her hands and on her cheeks, there had been the taste and the smell of an almost childlike sense of desolation. She had been quite unable to keep up any pretense, and when people she met and looked at with a haggard and a hunted eye had asked her what was wrong, the mask had fallen from her face as though torn away by the very violence of her feelings. "Please leave me alone," she had groaned; "it's nothing: it will pass"—though not, for a moment, imagining that anything could ever again bring balm to a torment, rather than endure which, she would choose to die.

Fabien went up to her, took her hand, and shyly asked whether the Princess would include him in her invitation.

"You must be mad! She detests you. . . . She thinks of you as my murderer! Besides, I'm going away to get cured, and it's of you I've got to get cured. . . ."

She freed her hand and moved across to the other side of the bed, so as to put a space between them. She remembered the time when the mere proximity of his body had set her trembling, so that her teeth had chattered and her hands grown cold.

"Fabien, I'm going to show you that I'm not such a cat as you think me. I have news of Colombe. . . ."

"Ah!"

"Donald doesn't like the idea of leaving her at the Convent. It seems that she is passing through a highly emotional stage of religiosity, and he's afraid the good Sisters may put ideas into her head."

He said nothing, and she went on:

"As a matter of fact, Thérèse is the only likely obstacle. I think I can persuade Donald without much difficulty. . . . Rather than see his daughter turn nun, as she seems bent on doing . . . after all, it wouldn't be at all a bad match for her, and I'm beginning to think that an affectionate and pious young girl might succeed in making you very happy."

"But what about you, Fanny?"

"Oh, I surrender all claims. I am prepared to go right out of your life. You will have been the last storm that I shall ever suffer. . . . I shall know what real peace means . . . the calm of smooth water after the buffetings of the gale! . . ."

But the flame of his youth refused to burn low, refused to come to terms with such extremities of wisdom. There was a mad look in his eyes as he strode across to the bed and imprisoned her in his arms as in a snare. She dared not struggle, but, inert and clearheaded, lay watching the young man who had once been so spoiled and indolent, and was now embarrassed, awkward in attack, and quelled by her coldness. She laughed, covering her eyes with her arm, and there was a note of uncontrolled hysteria in the sound such as he remembered to have heard when, long ago, on Christmas night, he had been kissed for the first time in the dark old house. . . . At last she grew calmer. Letting fall the arm that covered her face, she breathed out a sigh. She felt numbed but free. She was alone.

Fabien must have spent that night wandering along the deserted river bank near the Champ de Mars and the Magic City. It was not raining, but his clothing was drenched with mist. Just before dawn he found himself at his own door. Fumblingly he undressed, and when morning came was shivering with fever. When the maid arrived to do his room he asked her to put a jug of milk and some aspirin on the table, and leave him to sleep. He had always looked on illness as a soporific drug, a strange world in which he could lose himself, a road beckoning him to a rest without end. Who was it that had said to him that action is but another form of sleep? The restless persons of this world are but sleepers. Real life lies elsewhere. The odd thing was that he felt neither anxiety nor remorse. He kept on repeating to himself a single line of poetry: *Puisque c'est si peu nous qui faisons notre vie.* He felt deep sunk in security because nobody, nobody at all, would come. He had to struggle for his breath. Had he, perhaps, developed congestion of the lungs? He lay struck down by the weight of a deadening slumber, shot through with a sense of something that was almost dreaming, only to sink once more into a sort of burning torpor. Somebody, a man, opened the door. He saw Maïnz taking off his overcoat. He closed his eyes, making believe he slept. A cool hand was laid upon his forehead and fingers pressed his wrist. He heard Maïnz whispering on the landing, telling somebody the address of a doctor.

That night, after the doctor had gone, he opened his eyes and saw in an armchair the figure of the Jew whom he knew so little, watching beside his bed. At dawn it was still there, and came across to lift his head that he might drink. Another day the sick man opened his eyes and saw his mother. She leaned down to kiss him, and he recognized the mingled smell of lavender, naphtha balls and orris root which had always hung about the room where he and Joseph had said their evening prayers. Later, he was conscious of a priest whispering in his ear.

"A woman, my son?"

He made a sign of assent with his eyes.

"Married?"

"Yes. . . ."

The priest said: "I will return . . . offer up your life . . . Our Lord . . . your sufferings. . . ."

They gave him an injection of serum through the pleura,

right into the affected lung. No one knew that he was rejoicing at his sufferings. Maïnz was talking to Madame Dézaymeries at the window. Fabien stirred, moved his lips, and at last was able to articulate:

"Maïnz——"

When the Jew leaned down above the bed, he made a supreme effort and managed to say:

"Don't judge the tree . . . rotten fruit. . . ."

He could say no more, and it occurred to Maïnz that Christ, maybe, had chosen to reveal Himself in the weakest of His vessels.

When he went down to dinner, Madame Dézaymeries put a question:

"Have you sent word to the college authorities?"

"There's no need; he sent in his resignation a month ago."

She showed no sign of amazement. Left to herself she gazed at the man she thought she had known so well. He lay now sleeping peacefully. The doctor had said that injections made directly into the lung can sometimes work miracles. When she had prepared the table for the Last Sacrament (which was to be brought during the night) she kneeled down. Her lips moved, but she could attach no meaning to her words. That morning she had found, tucked away in a drawer, a number of hairpins and a light-colored tortoise-shell comb. *"Third Sorrowful Mystery. . . . Where was I?"* Fabien heard, as once in his childhood's dreaming, the click of the rosary which Madame Dézaymeries was holding like a skein of wool so as to be sure‛ how far she had got in her "telling." But she found it impossible to concentrate on her devotions. She got up and took down from a shelf what she thought was her son's prayer book.

But it turned out to be a small photograph album. She took it to the light, opened it, and turned the pages without making a sound, though she must have read the legends inscribed beneath each picture: *Fanny at the Lido; Fanny on the Piazetta; Fanny at San Francesco-del-Deserto; Our Gondolier; Our Room.*

Quite calmly she put the album back and kneeled down by the bed. She stayed there as motionless as though her body had been turned to stone. Her hollow cheeks had the gray color of stone. At intervals she said, in a low voice, but very distinctly, "On me alone, on me alone. May it all be laid on me." She was remembering the little girl whom she had welcomed, forty years ago, in the old Dupouy house, and how she had loved her frivolity, her impertinent ways, her wild fits of temper. "Was it not for those very vices, then scarcely developed, that she was dear to me, though I did not know it? No, I *did* know it, and later, when I took her in, I did not deceive myself. I refused to see that even then she was prowling around Fabien. Oh, please God let him live, if, by living, he may make atonement. But let him die if death will open the gates of heaven to him. But may Thy justice fall on me alone, miserable sinner that I am."

Fabien still lay dozing. His nose was no longer twitching as it had been earlier, his hand upon the sheet was no longer flushed to a dark red. Thérèse heard a sound of whispering on the stairs, and, thinking it was the Sacrament, lit the two candles on the table that was covered with a cloth. She opened the door and took from the servant a light wicker basket addressed to Fabien Dézaymeries. The name on the card—Madame Donald Larsen —meant nothing to her, but even after all these years she recognized the thin, firm writing of the message that accompanied it: "From the happy land in which I have been born anew, I send to dear Fabien a thought of loyal affection." She tore the card into small pieces and threw them on the fire together with the paper in which the flowers had been wrapped. A flame leapt up. Then she thrust into the blaze great handfuls of gilliflowers, mimosa and carnations, their stalks still wet, that they, too, might be consumed.

At that moment a young priest arrived. There was a devout expression on his face by reason of what he was carrying beneath his cloak. Thérèse dropped to her knees, still holding some flowers in her hand. For a moment she hesitated, then strewed them on the table and the carpet. The priest trod them under his muddy shoes. It was necessary to rouse Fabien. He said that he felt better, and that there was a smell of crushed flowers in the room. His mother wrapped him in a shawl and supported his body while he stretched his waxen face to the Host. The quiet smile never left his lips. God was still in him when he sank once more into sleep. As the priest withdrew he noticed Maïnz standing outside the door, because he had not dared to enter the room.

All that night Madame Dézaymeries watched by her son as he lay sleeping peacefully. She thought that, maybe, the breast that has quivered with the ecstasies of passion had been chosen, as once had been the rim of a well, a publican's table, and that place of sin where the Son of Man had eaten and drunk because he had been sent to call sinners to repentance.

Toward the end of the spring it became possible to move Fabien to the heath country where the sun was already overpowering. From the month of June onward the cicadas made it impossible for anyone to do more than slumber uneasily, and only when with the coming of evening the woods distilled their scent, did sleep come. As darkness deepened the air was filled with the smell of burned heather and brackish water. The Dézaymeries' were expecting a visit from Jacques Maïnz at the end of July. One morning Fabien's mother gave him a letter from Fanny.

He said, averting his eyes: "What ought I to do?"

Perhaps he was thinking that he had in charge a human soul, that sin sometimes binds us to another like a Sacrament.

Madame Dézaymeries thought for a moment before replying:

"We are of those who believe that a soul may be influenced at a distance by prayer and sacrifice."

She said no more, but the light of a great joy showed in her face as she watched the young man tear up the letter without so much as opening it. For a while after this frequent letters arrived from Fanny because Fabien made no effort to reply. It became a habit with him to tear them all up unread. For this seeming cruelty he should not be too harshly judged. In order that his mistress might be saved he had refused to open his heart to the call of human happiness, and already he was dead to the world. But for all his resolution the claims of the body could not be altogether stilled. For long months it had been gorged, how then, when it had once more woken to life, could it be kept from craving satisfaction? The real story of Fabien Dézaymeries should, properly speaking, begin at this point, for all that had gone before was in the nature of a prologue. But how is one to describe the secret drama of a man who struggles to subdue his earthy heritage, that drama which finds expression neither in words nor gestures? Where is the artist who may dare to imagine the processes and shifts of the great protagonist —Grace? It is the mark of our slavery and of our wretchedness that we can, without lying, paint a faithful portrait only of the passions.

9 780374 526498